大展好書 好書大展

大展好書 好書大展

語文特輯20

American idiomatic Expressions and Conversation

藥學碩士 王嘉明 著

大展出版社有限公司

序 (1)

王嘉明先生請我為這本書寫序時，我有特別的感受。

前幾天，正好厚生基金會頒發醫療奉獻獎，得獎的多是外藉人士。這麼多位外籍朋友長年為台灣無私奉獻，高貴的情操令人感動。其中一位蘭醫師，兩代在彰化服務，聽到他用流利的閩南語（台灣地區語言之一）致詞，我深感他們對語言之用心學習，運用自如，是對另一種文化的尊重與認識。

語言是很迷人的。優雅用詞，必需學習；俗用俚語如能體會，則更深一層。我大學畢業後，在國外住了二十幾年，有時仍然對電視上的美式笑話，不能百分之百體會，語言是要永續學習。

世界村是趨勢，精通其他語言，則有進入新境界的感受，語言的魅力是何等深遠！

王嘉明先生是北醫藥學系傑出校友，後來負笈新英格蘭。回國後，除經營本行業務，更熱心參與社會服務。此書是他「推己及人」，與各位朋友分享他的心得，內容豐富實用，我欣見此書出版，特為之序。

胡俊弘

一九九六、二、廿七

臺北醫學院校長

史丹福大學醫學院皮膚科學教授

序 (2)

國人從小就接受英文（語）教育，一般人對於英文閱讀，多能應付自如，尤其是參加托福之類的考試，更是得心應手，但在與外國人來往時，卻常有「說不出」、「聽不懂」的困擾。值此政府積極推動重返國際社會的時刻，如何學會使用國際語言——英語，實為一重要課題。

藥師公會社區藥局主任委員王嘉明藥師，是留美的藥學碩士，在工作之餘，將留美期間學習英語的心得撰成「學會美式俚語會話」一書，以最淺顯的方式介紹在書本、字典上不常出現，但卻是日常會話中常用的俚語，幫助讀者抓住說英語的訣竅，使讀者在最短的時間內，能夠開口說英語。書中並提到「美語三字經」，這類語言雖然不雅，但在日常生活中、電影對白裡卻常可聽到，我們雖不去使用，但卻應該加以認識。

王藥師不是英語科班出身，因此能擺脫僵化嚴肅的教條，而以真實、生活化的方式來教導讀者學習英語。「學會美式俚語會話」一書，內容精彩、簡淺而不落俗套，將能使有心學習說英語者更具信心，尤其是對於學習多年而仍無法開口者，必能提供莫大助益。

立法委員 洪秀柱

序 (3)

拜科技進步之賜，人類環遊世界的夢想得以容易實現。國際間的接觸因而逐漸增加，關係也更加緊密。在即將邁入廿一世紀的同時，世界儼然已成為一個地球村，天涯若比鄰，國際間溝通的橋樑最常用的語言「英語」也更形重要，同時為了因應新資訊時代國際網路的來臨，更是非學好英語不可。

由於經常出國接洽業務，也都以英語為主，對英語也曾下過苦功，對英語的學習有更深的體認。開拓業務時語言的溝通能夠了解，加深彼此間的印象，拉近彼此間的距離。在國內有多位學者曾指出台灣英語教育制度僵化，學校英語教學以考試為主，只重視文法、單字，而忽視日常口語化的教材活用，以致於學生雖擁有良好的英語閱讀能力，卻仍無法說出口。比起香港、新加坡、菲律賓，說英語在台灣仍不夠普及。所以在政府大力推動國際化的過程中產生很大的問題。可見國人對於英語的讀、寫方面沒有問題，反而是日常英語會話和聽力方面的障礙。

本書適時的提供讀者增進聽力和開口說英語的最佳學習方法。沒有教條式的冗繁，舉例簡淺，更務實化、更生活化、更人性化是學習英語最佳教材。英語是國際間溝通的橋樑，也是學習知識的重要工具，王君除在專業領域鑽研之外，對英語研究的用心，更是值得鼓勵與肯定，余樂為序推薦。

中華民國藥師公會全國聯合會
理事長 [signature]

序 (4)

科學日新月異、工商日益進步，科技縮短了人與人之間的有形距離；人與人之交往頻繁，國與國之間之關係日益密切。尤其台灣經濟發達，國民所得提高，人們到國外旅遊或經商機會多了，免不了要用國際語言──英語，但是我們從小學甚至幼稚園即開始學到大學畢業，都在學英語，甚至工作上很多資料仍是英文。但是有幾人能說一口流利的英文呢？有一些人移民到美國、加拿大十多年了，仍然是五子登科「啞子」！是什麼原因呢？嘉明兄將告訴您為何不敢開口的原因。

嘉明兄不務正業在執業藥局之餘，將留美期間俚語叢書、電視、電影及日常生活雜記有系統的整理，完成了簡單扼要、易懂易學『學會美式俚語會話』一書，此書生活化、活潑化、趣味化；讓您開口說美語不難，希望藉此書，讓學多年英語不敢講的人茅塞頓開，更希望讓初學者，有啟蒙作用。熟讀此書，旅遊歐美無語言障礙，商務會話無往不利。順祝讀者得心順口如您所願！

臺北市藥師公會
理事長 張森賢

自 序

學習英語已成為世界潮流，根據統計全世界說英語的人口約有五億人，會說英語使你不論出國留學、商務考察、觀光旅遊世界無往不利，就業順利。目前政府大力推動經濟自由化、國際化的同時，學好英語更是必須的。我國人從國中、高中，乃至大學，學習英語數十年，但對多數人而言，仍有說不出口和聽不懂的遺憾。甚至有人以為到了美國這個英語國家的大染缸，英語就自然而然的進步神速，事實並非如此。你也許不相信在美國住了二十年的老華僑仍說著家鄉話，吃著中國菜。

學習語言沒有速成，而是須要正確的學習方法，不斷的背誦和反覆的練習。現在國內一般人所聽到的、用到的、講的都是以美式英語為主，而一般美國人日常所說的英語會話，有時在書本上或字典上卻很少見到，但卻是平日常用的。有時字面上意義很簡單，但實際意義卻又不盡相同。

例如：1. That problem is a piece of cake for her;She's an expert in that field.

那問題對她而言太容易了；她是那方面的專家。

〔註〕a piece of cake，指非常容易，即 very easy。為【非正式】用語。

2. come on, gimme a break,I can't do a hundred things at the same time.

算了，饒了我吧，我不可能同時做好幾件事的。

〔註〕gimme a break 即 give me a break

饒了我吧或別開玩笑了。制止別人的揶揄或說風涼話。

3.Joan:What are we gonna do?

Matt:Let's split.

Joan:我們該怎麼辦?

Matt:我們快離開。

〔註〕(1) gonna 是 going to 之縮寫連音，相同

I've gotta go.

即 I've got to go. 我必須離開了。

(2) split，【俚語】，突然離開，走開。

相信對大衆多數和留學生而言，初抵美國時都有同樣的困惑，「鴨仔聽雷」，為此原故著者乃根據留美期間擷取各美俚語、俗語叢書和每日課餘勤看電視，以及日常生活中「道」聽「途」說的生活點滴所記錄下的筆記，經整理並承蒙發行人蔡森明先生的協助出版，希望對有心學好英語人士有所助益。讓你不論看電影、電視影集、出國留學、觀光旅遊、工商考察，說英語更能得心應手。

筆者並非語言專家，大膽著書，乃將學習心得，公諸於斯，無非希望拋磚引玉，激起有心學好英語人士說英語就像說國語一樣也會通，「我能，你也能」的共鳴。本書的寫成，雖經仔細斧正，疏漏之處難免，仍請不吝指正。

王嘉明

1996年2月1日

序於台北

目　　錄

第三篇 美語三字經

第四篇 附 錄

第一篇

開口說英語不難—學會說英語的訣竅

1-1　活用簡單的基本動詞

1-2　熟記常用慣用語

1-3　加強聽力的方法—養成記摘要的習慣

1-4　以英語說英語—勿以中文聯想

1-5　學好正確發音

1-6　多聽多講多練習

第一篇　開口說英語不難

—學會說英語的訣竅

隨著社會繁榮，國人出國機會增多，國際間接觸頻繁，英語便成為世人共同的語言，但很多人礙於時間或學習方法，無法如願學會說英語。其實學會說英語並不難，但要說得字正腔圓有深度可就不那麼容易。學了多年英語，開口說英語是每個人的願望，但對多數人而言，總有說不出口和聽不懂的遺憾。雖然經歷了大小英語考試以至留學托福考試，在英語讀和寫方面有很好的根基，但每當和外國人交談時，卻常有舌頭打結，有口難言的痛苦，或者「鴨仔聽雷」有聽沒有懂，這是因為你對口語化英語的了解和別人對你所說英語口音的了解仍有困難之故。學習語言沒有速成，而是須要正確的學習方法，不斷的背誦和反覆的練習，讀者如能按照下列幾項學習的方法，按步就班，學會開口說英語不難。

1-1　活用簡單的基本動詞

讀英語和說英語不同，說英語時應盡量的說簡潔的，口語化的英語，愈簡單愈好。其實只要能活用簡單的基本動詞，國中程度便可說流利的英語。本書的用意是教你如何開口說英語，所以說簡潔的英語，愈簡單愈好。例如 do, let, give, get take, keep…等基本動詞，連國中生都懂，但對多數學英語的人士，像大學生、上班族、家庭主婦或其他各界人士，往往忽略了它的功用，而捨近求遠。其實學會基本動詞的許多含意和用法，便容易開口說英語，舉例如下：簡單動詞的多種用途。

1.【have】的多種用法

〔註1.〕有

a. I have a house in the country.
我在鄉間有一幢房子。

b. I have a word with you.
我有話對你說。

〔註2.〕取用，獲得

May I have another cup of coffee?
我可以再要一杯咖啡嗎？

〔註3.〕令，使

a. I must have my hair cut.
我必須要理髮了。

b. Please have Bob bring these things to my house.
請派 Bob 將這些東西搬到我家。

〔註4.〕與 to 連用，當必須。have to 表示 must

a. you don't have to go.
你不須要去。

b. In order to pass Exam,I have to study hard.
為了通過考試，我必須努力用功。

2.【do】的多種用法

〔註1.〕用於疑問句

Do you feel cold today?
今天你覺得很冷嗎？

〔註2.〕加強動詞語氣

Please do stay.

請務必留下。

〔註3.〕用於表示否定時

Don't go away!

請別走開!(Do not go away!)

〔註4.〕做(指動作)

What are you doing now?

你正在幹啥?

〔註5.〕盡力而為

I'll do my best.

我將盡力而為。

〔註6.〕處理,料理,整理

The maid will do your room.

女傭會幫你整理房間。

3.【get】的用法

〔註1.〕抵達,到達

a. I'll soon get to Boston.

我將很快抵達波士頓。

b. A: Will you tell me when we get 42 street, please.

B: Don't worry! I'll tell you when we get there.

A: 當到達 42 街時請告訴我。

B: 別擔心!當我們到達時我會告訴你的。

〔註2.〕取,拿給

Get me a hammer from the kitchen, will you?

到廚房拿把鐵鎚給我,好嗎?

〔註3.〕明白,了解

a. Got it?

知道了嗎?

b. I can't get what you mean.

我不明白你的意思。

〔註4.〕同become，漸漸變成

The weather is getting cold.

天氣漸漸變冷了。

想不到以上這些簡單的動詞也有這麼多功能的用法。

1-2　熟記常用慣用語(idioms)

現在國內一般人所聽到的，用到的講的英語會話都是以美式英語為主，而一般美國人日常所說的英語會話，有時在書本上或字典上卻很少見到，但卻是平日常用的，有時字面上意義很簡單，但實際意義卻又不盡相同，這是由於慣用語的關係。舉例如下:

1. all set

〔註〕指好了，準備好了，即 all ready，finish 之意。

例: Are you all set?

你做好了嗎?

I'm all set.

我好了。

2. beat it 走開，滾開

〔註〕【俚語】不客氣的口氣，get out,go away.

3. cop 警察

〔註〕【非正式】用語，指警察，條子。是歹徒最痛恨的剋星，其他尙有稱警察爲

pig, officer, police, policeman, smokey。

例：Cops come on the way.

警察馬上就到。

4. cut it out

停止，別再說了。

〔註〕阻止別人說風涼話或揶揄。同 knock it off。

5. check it out

去查明白。查看一下。

〔註〕同 To look。常用口語。與 Check out 意義不同。

6. do up 弄好；扣起；束起

〔註〕**【俗語】非常廣用**

例1.：Do up your coat.

扣好你的外衣。

例2.：Will you do up my dress at the back, please.

請替我把衣服背後扣子扣好。

7. give me a break

饒了我吧；別拿我開玩笑。

〔註〕制止別人的揶揄或說風涼話。

8. go for it

做吧；盡力；盡全力做好。

A: I want to buy a car.

B: Go for it.

A: 我要買部車子。

B: 去買吧。

9. Long time no see

好久不見了。

10. a piece of cake

太容易了。

〔註〕【非正式】用語；very easy，指非常容易做的事。

11. Set up

陷害

例：He was set up.

他被陷害了。

12. Sure thing

當然的。

〔註〕【非正式】用語，即 of course；Centainly

例：Sure thing, I'll be glad to do it for you.

當然，我很樂意為你效勞。

13. you bet

當然；一定

〔註〕【非正式】用語，強調事實就是如此。

例1.：You bet,I will.

當然我會的。

2.：You bet I will be at the party.

我一定參加宴會的。

以上所舉的例子也許你會覺得很陌生，但請勿猶豫，把它背下來，因為這是美式會話常會用到的，本書第二篇將再詳加介紹。

1-3　加強聽力的方法－養成記摘要的習慣（Note-taking）

無法開口說英語，障礙之一是聽不懂，所以必須加強聽力訓練是很重要的。如何增強聽力？學記摘要是最有效的方法。留學生上課除了數理科較多理解計算有書本可參考外，像醫學、藥學、法律、企管之類課程專業術語甚多，除了聽講還要記筆記，討論，常會「鴨仔聽雷」苦不堪言。記摘要是相當重要的，因為你會專心什麼該記，什麼不該記，而且有助於聽力的訓練。你應該記下最重要部份的字，以及那些字所代表重要的意義和資訊等，例如名詞、動詞、數目、統計數、日期、人名、地點等這些字叫含意字（content words），有些字像冠詞the, an, so forth, 介詞等可不必記下即結構字（structure words）。舉例如下：The president of the United States arrived back in Washing, D.C. late in the evening of Monday,July6.（美國總統七月六日星期一午夜回到華盛頓D.C.）本句可摘記如下，濃縮後意義不變。即 President United States arrived D.C. Monday July 6. 摘要記錄方式如下：Pres. U.S. arriv. D.C. Mon 7/ 6. 平常若能養成記摘要的習慣，試著利用時間在紙上用最簡單，最迅速的方法，記錄有關聽到的年、月、日時間、地點、長度、數據等重要資料，對於會話聽力的加強，應付托福聽力測驗、商業談判或會議討論等有很大的幫助。

【常用簡化記號】

1.＝ equals 相等，等於
2.≒ does not equal 不等
3.＞ is greater than 大於
4.＜ is less than 小於
5.→ causes;results in 導致
6.← is caused by;resulted in 起因於
7.re about;concerning 關於
8.eg for example 例如

9.ie　that is;for example(also)即是

10.∴　therefore 所以

11.$　money 金錢

12.%　percent 百分比

13.&　and 和

14.+　plus 加

1-4　以英語說英語—勿以中文聯想

對多數人而言，說英語的阻礙是想好中文再轉換成英文，想隨口說英語應以英文聯想直接說出。舉例如下：

1. 想用英語說一句「我知道了」，「我明白了」用英語怎麼說呢？

(1) I see.

(2) I know.

(3) I understand.

(4) I've got it.

(5) I've got the point.

(6) I've got the picture.

這麼簡單的中文，竟有這麼多的英語表達方式，你會大吃一驚吧！

2. 「她懷孕了」。

She have pregrant. 懷孕 pregrant 單字一時想不出來，應以其他簡單的方式聯想表示意思一樣。

例 She is having a baby.

3. 「機械運轉得很好」，運轉，轉動 run，你是否想到亦可以用 work 取代。

a. The machine is running well.

b. The machine is working well.

4. 「你開我玩笑。」

① You put me on.

② You're kidding me.

③ You're pulling my leg.

英語的表達方式有各種不同的方法，所以說英語時儘量以最簡單的方式避免使用艱深難懂的單字，說的人難過，聽的人也迷糊。

1-5 學好正確發音

聽英語和說英語不同，當美國人說英語時，我們可以聽得懂，因為聽的時候祇要大致了解便可以聽懂，但要和他們一樣字正腔圓的發音可就不容易，中國學生最不容易的音像 s, θ b, v, r, l 等，發音不正確常失之毫釐差之千里，導致別人對你所說英語的難以了解，要使自己發音正確，平常要多練習基本的發音。由於美式英語風行全球，國內一般人所聽到的，講的英語也是以美式英語為主，所以務必學好K.K音標的發音。

Ⅰ. 中國學生較容易弄混的發音

1. [f] 與 [v] 的區別

[f] 上齒含著下唇，聲帶不震動，近似國語注音的〔ㄈ〕

例：fought [fɔt] 打仗

food [fud] 食物

feet [fit] 腳

[v] 上齒咬著下唇，聲帶震動，國語無此音

例：very ['vɛrɪ] 非常，很。

vote［vot］投票

2. ［p］與［b］的區別

［p］雙唇音，聲帶不震動，近似國語的〔ㄆ〕

例：peep［pip］窺視

pen［pεn］筆

［b］雙唇音，聲帶震動，近似國語的〔ㄅ〕

例：boat［bot］船

body［'badi］身體

3. ［r］與［l］之區別

［r］捲舌音，聲帶振動，在字首時近似國語注音的〔ㄖ〕，而摩擦較輕，在字尾時近似［ㄦ］

right［rait］右邊　　door［dɔr］門

rate［ret］比率　　chair［tʃεr］椅子

［l］舌尖頂住上顎，聲帶震動，近似國語的〔ㄌ〕

例：ball［bɔl］球

Look［'luk］看

4. ［θ］與［ð］的區別

［θ］上下齒含著舌尖，聲帶不震動，讓氣息從舌尖和上齒間的空隙中流出，國語無此音

例：think［θɪŋk］想

thank［θæŋk］謝謝

［ð］上下齒含著舌尖，聲帶震動，國語無此音

例：Mother［'mʌðɚ］母親

there［'ðεr］那裡

II. 注意重音的位置

英文字重音位置大致不是在第一音節，就是在第二音節，第三音節的字較少，較易發錯音。重音不對影響正確的發音，溝通產生困難。

例：recommend ［rekemend］ 推薦
guarautee［gærənti；］ 保證
employee ［ ɪmplɔɪi］ 職員，被雇員工
shampoo ［ ʃæmpu］ 洗髮精
volunteer ［vɔləntiə ］ 自願
millionaire ［miljənɛə］ 百萬富翁
comprehend ［kəmprihend］ 了解

1-6 多聽多講多練習

會話時只要不太離譜，不要太在意文法，不要害怕錯誤，多開口練習。縱使發音不是很好，也要大聲說出。在國內可每日看中國郵報（China post）和收聽台北國際社區電台（I.C.R.T.）節目或 CNN 電視台，電視影集，對於會話時，聽力的增進會有很大的幫助。會話時即使無人可練習，亦可自己朗讀英語會話，例如英語九百句型，可隨課本大聲朗讀，並記住常用句型，反覆練習，對開口說英語將有莫大的助益。

第二篇
常用美式俚語

2-1 每個單字都了解，為什麽會聽不懂—

學了多年英語，開口說英語是每個人的願望。但對多數人而言，雖然經歷了大小英語考試以至通過留學托福考試（TOEFL），但當你初抵美國留學時，仍會有「鴨仔聽雷」的痛苦，對口說英語的了解和別人對你所說英語的了解仍有困難，原因之一是不熟悉慣用語（Idioms）。

什麽是慣用語（Idioms）？

如果在英語會話時或在書本上，你了解每一個單字，但卻無法抓住它真正的意思，八成是你對慣用語（Idioms）了解有困難。

簡言之，慣用語通常是指由一組字組成，它有自己特別的意義。像 slang（俚語），colloquial（俗語），Informal（非正式用語）等。

〔**實例**〕：Tom is a real cool cat,His hair is pepper and salt but he knows how to make up for lost time by taking it easy. He get up early,works out, and turns in early.

Tom 是一位很冷靜的人，他頭髮灰白，但他知道放鬆自己來補償失去的時間。他早起，做運動，並且早睡。

【**註解**】：1. cool cat 指很冷靜，沉著的人

2. pepper and salt 指白色黑色交雜頭髮，即灰色頭髮

3. make up 補償

4. take it easy 放輕鬆，relax，別緊張之意。

※5. work out 做運動

※6. turn in 上床睡覺

不用說這並不是很正式的英語，但對大部份美國人而言，當他們交談時常以此種方式表達。

對於外國學生而言，實在很難了解此種美國式的英語會話，縱使你對文法很了解也於事無補。

Idioms一般可分為三類：

Ⅰ. lexemic Idioms：這類 idioms 較易區別出來與熟悉的說話部份有關聯，它可能是動詞片語，如 get up 起床，work out 運動，turn in 上床睡覺。名詞片語，如 hot dog 熱狗，White House 白宮。形容詞片語，如 pepper and salt 灰白頭髮。

Ⅱ. phrase idioms：較長的 idioms，可能是一個句子，與文法沒有相連關係，在美式英語中佔大部份。

例：1. Kick the bucket （即 die; pass away）
死去。

2. piece of cake （即 very easy）
很簡單，很容易。

Ⅲ. proverbial idioms：即 saying 或 proverbs.
格言或諺語。

例：Blood is thicker than water.
血濃於水（比喻骨肉親情之深）

任何人想學好英語，使之更流利更道地，如何正確使用 idioms 也是很重要的，你不但要學 native speaker 的口語法，更須注意使用程度的限制。

註：【slang】，俚語，此種 idiom 用於親近或彼此較熟悉的朋友，但會話時卻廣為使用。

【colloquial】俗語，如 movie 是 moving picture 的俗語。

【Informal】非正式用語，此種形式常見於口語會話，但正式文章則避免使用。

【formal】正式用語，較正式用語，常見於寫作，演說或文學上。

2-2　常用美式俚語

【說明】

為便於查閱，本篇按照字母順序，收錄許多常用俚語，俗語，非正式用語，以及常用會話短句。且日常生活會話中最常用語，則加註有※記號，加深讀者印象，請勿猶豫把它背起來。

每一俚語或俗語並加註例句，供讀者練習參考。

2-3 PART(A)

Ⅰ. 常用單字，俚語，俗語，非正式用語

1. Ambulance 救護車

['æmbjələns]

※2. Attorney 律師，代辯人

〔註〕：Lawyer 律師

plaintiff ['plentif] n.原告

defendant [di'fɛndənt] n.被告

you honor 庭上

例：The plaintiff accused the defendant of fraud.

原告控訴被告犯詐欺罪。

※3. Absolutely 絕對的，肯定地

〔註〕：【俚語】，正是如此。常用於肯定的口語。

例1. Absolutely no way 絕對不可行的

2. Absolutely,he is right.

我肯定，他是對的。

4. alternative 選擇，指二個可能中之一，亦可從數個中選擇其一的。

〔註〕：同option,choice

例1. There are several alternative routes from Boston to New York.

從波士頓到紐約有好幾條路可選擇。

2. It's my option.

這是我的選擇。

5. announcer

〔註〕：指電視播音員，電視記者。D.J.（Disc Joekey）則是指無線電台廣播員。

※6. available 有用的，可利用的，有效的

例：The round trip ticket is available for a month.
來回車票一個月有效。

※7. Appreciate 感激，感謝

[ə'priʃɪˏet]

〔註〕常用於口語，同Thank，對別人表示感謝。

例1. I'll appreciate.
我會很感激的。

例2. I appreciate your kindness.
我感謝您的好意。

8. a bit

〔註〕：【非正式】用語，一點點，指很少量。
a little bit 有一些。

例1：There's no sugar in the sugar bowl, but you may find a bit in the bag.
碗裡沒有糖了，但你可在袋子裡找到一些。

例2：If the ball had hit the window a bit harder, it would have broken it.
如果球再撞窗戶大力一點，它可能就打破了。

例3：A：Have some more cake?
再吃些餅干嗎？
B：Thanks. A bit more won't hurt me.
謝謝。再多一點對我無妨。

9. about time.

〔註〕：名詞片語，指該是時候了，最後時刻

例句1：Mother said,"It's about time you got up,Mary."

母親說"瑪麗，該是起床的時刻了。"

例句2："The basketball team won last night. About time."

棒球對昨晚贏了，正是時機。

10. about to

〔註〕：指即將，正準備去。be about to

例1. I haven't gone yet,but I'm about to.

我尚未離開，但即將出發。

例2. I was about to leave when the secretary showed up.

當秘書出現時，我正準備離開。

例3. We were about to leave when the snow began.

當開始下雪時，我們正準備離開。

※11. according to

〔註〕：根據，依據

例1. According to the Bible,Adam was the first. man.

根據聖經，亞當是第一位男人。

例2. Many words are pronounced according to the spelling but some are not.

許多字的發音是根據拼音，但有些不是。

※12. act out

〔註1〕付諸行動

例：All his life he tried to act out his beliefs.
他傾一生對他的信仰付諸行動。

〔註2〕表達思想，故事，或你臉上表情，談話動作。

例：He tried to act out a story that he had read.
他試著表達他讀過故事的內容。

13. act up

〔註1〕【非正式】用語，指粗魯行為，粗魯動作。

例：The dog acted up as the postman came to the door.
當郵差走到門口時，狗粗魯的吼叫。

〔註2〕指機器作用運作不好

例：The car acted up because the spark plugs were dirty.
由於火星塞不乾淨，車子跑得不順。

14. add up

〔註1〕：【非正式】用語，即To make sense，合理的，可以理解的。

例：His story didn't add up.
他的故事不近情理。

〔註2〕：add up to 加到…總數，數量。

例：The bill added up to $12.95.
鈔票加起來是美金12.95元。

〔註3〕達到正確數量

例：The numbers wouldn't add up.
這些數目加不起來（不合）。

15. ahead of time

〔註〕副詞片語，指比預定時間早

例：The bus came ahead of time, and Mary was not ready.
公車來早了，Mary 尚未準備好。

例：The new building was finished ahead of time.
新大厦比預定時間提早蓋好。

※16. air shuttle (n.)

〔註〕：【俗語】空中巴士，指在兩個距離不太遠的主要城市定期服務的航空班機。
如波士頓到紐約，此種班機不必事先訂位。
shuttle bus 則是定時來回近距離兩地的公共汽車。

例：My dad takes the air shuttle from Bostom to New York once a week. 我爹地每星期一次搭空中巴士來回波士頓、紐約之間。

17. after hours (副詞片語)

〔註〕：指非正常或平常期間。繼續或正常時間以後開門營業。

例1. The store was clearned and swept out after hours.
商店在正常打烊時間後清潔打掃。

例2. The children had a secret after hours party when they were supposed to be in bed.
應該上床睡覺的時間小孩子們有一秘密舞會。

18. after a while (or in a while)

〔註〕：【非正式】副詞片語，指稍後不久，待會兒。

例1. Q：Dad, will you help me make this model plane?

爹地，請幫我做模型飛機好嗎？

A：After a while, Son, when I finish reading the newspaper.

兒子，待會兒，等我看完報紙吧。

例2. The boys gathered some wood, and in a while, a hot fire was burning.

男孩子們收集了一些木材，不久之後熊熊烈火即燃燒著。

19. all at once

〔註1〕：副詞片語，同時地，在同一時間

例1. Bill can play the piano, sing, and lead his orchestra all at once.

Bill 能同時彈鋼琴，唱歌，演奏管絃樂。

〔註2〕：意同all of a sudden 突然地

例1. All at once we heard a shot and the soldier fell to the ground.

突然間我們聽到射擊聲，士兵應聲倒地。

例2. All of a sudden the ship struck a rock.

突然間船撞到岩石。

※20. all ears

〔註〕：洗耳恭聽　【非正式】用語，指非常熱切聽到，非常注意。

例1. Go ahead with your story; we are all ears.

儘管說你的故事吧，我們洗耳恭聽。

例2. When John told about the circus, the boys were all ears.

當 John 談論馬戲團的事，孩子們都專心傾聽。

21. all kind of

〔註〕：形容詞片語，【非正式】用語，plenty of，各種不同的，充滿著，很豐富的。

例1. When Kathy was sick,she had all kind of company.

當 Kathy 生病時，她有許多不同的同伴。

例2. People say that Mr. Fox has all kinds of money.

人們說 Fox 先生很富有。

※22. all out

〔註〕：副詞片語【非正式】用法，指使盡全力，決心，通常使用go all out片語。

例1. We went all out to win the game.

我們使盡全力贏得比賽。

例2. John went all out to finish the job and was very tired afterwards.

John 使盡全力完成工作，最後倍感疲倦。

23. allow for

〔註〕：允許，給予機會，預留空間

例：Democracy allows for many differences of opinion.

民主政治允許表達各種不同的意見。

※24. all right 好的，好吧

〔註1〕：常用口語,好的,是的之意。用於歡呼時,很棒,太棒了,很好之意

例：Q：Shall we watch television?

A：All right.

問：我們可以看電視嗎？
答：好吧。
〔註2〕：指健康良好，精神很好
例1.Q：How are you？
A：I'm all right.
問：你好嗎？
答：我很好。
〔註3〕：足夠好，作用良好
例1. The new machine is running all right.
新機器運作良好。

※25. all set

〔註〕：常用口語。準備好了，做好了，做完了之意。即all done,all ready,finish之意。
例：Are you all set？
準備好沒有？
I'm all set.
我準備好了。

※26.a lot（n.）

〔註〕：【非正式】用語，常用於口語，指許多數量，許多，很多。very many or very much
例1. I learned a lot in Mr. Smith's class.
我在Smith先生班上學到很多。
例2. A lot of our friends are going to the beach this summer.
我們許多朋友今年暑假要到海邊去。

例3. Ella is a jolly girl;she laughs a lot.
Ella 是快樂女孩，她時常笑容滿面。

※27. answer for

〔註〕：負責任的，同take responsibility for.

例：The secret service has to answer for the safety of the president and his family.
秘密服務必須對總統和他家人負安全責任。

※28. apple polisher

〔註〕：指喜歡拍馬屁的人，馬屁精，即 butter someone up

※29. as follows

〔註〕：舉例如下，舉例說明時通常接：冒號

例1： My grocery list is as follows:bread,butter, meat,eggs,sugar.
我買的雜貨品項目如下：麵包，奶油，肉類，蛋，糖等。

例2. The names of the members are as follows: John Smith,Linda Long,Mary Webb.
會員名單如下：John Smith，Linda Long，Mary Webb。

※30. ask for

〔註〕：【非正式】用語，指自找麻煩，自找罪受。早告訴你阿花是虛情假意，你偏不聽，好了現在人財兩空，這是你自找的，you ask for it，活該！

※例1：You ask for it. 你自找罪受（怪不得別人）

例2. Charles drives fast on worn-out tires;he is

asking for trouble.

Charles使用壞的輪胎開快車，他是自找麻煩。

例3. Don't blame me, cause you ask for it.

別怪我，因為這是你自找的罪受。

※31. as soon as

〔註〕：conj連接詞，指即刻，立刻，儘快

例1. As soon as you finish your job let me know.

你一做完工作請讓我知道。

例2. He will see you as soon as he can.

他將儘快見你。

32. as well as

〔註〕：除外，also之意，也，除此之外也是。

例1. He was my friend as well as my doctor.

他是我的朋友也是我的醫師。

例2. Hiking is good exercise as well as fun.

遠足是一種好的運動而且也很有趣。

33. as usual

〔註〕：副詞片語，指像平常或往常一樣。

例：As usual, Tommy forget to make his bed before he went out to play.

跟平常一樣，Tommy出去玩之前又忘了摺被。

※34. at all costs

〔註〕：副詞片語，指不惜任何代價，時間，努力或金錢

例1. Carl is determined to succeed in his new job at all costs.

Carl決定不惜一切做好他新的工作。

例2. Mr. Jackson intended to save his son's eyesight at all costs.

Jackson先生不惜任何代價要挽回他兒子的視力。

35. at last

〔註〕：副詞片語，最後，終於

例1. The war had been long and hard,but now there was peace at last.

戰爭持續很久且艱苦，現在終於和平了。

※36. at least

〔註1〕：副詞片語，至少，不少於。

例1. You should brush your teeth at least twice a day.

你應該每天至少刷牙兩次。

例2. At least three students are failing in mathematics.

至少有三位學生算術不及格。

〔註2〕：不論如何，不管如何

例：She broke her arm,but at least it wasn't the arm she writes with.

她弄斷她的手，還好不管如何不是她寫字的那一隻手。

37. at leisure

〔註〕：副詞片語，空閒時間，閒暇時間。

例1. Come and visit us some evening when you're at leisure.

晚上有空時來看我們。

例2. John make the model plane at his leisure.

John在閒暇時間做好模型飛機。

38. at once

〔註〕：副詞片語，立刻之意，同immediately

例：Put a burning match next to a piece of paper,and it will being burning at once.
把燃燒的火柴放到一小紙片旁，它立刻燃燒。

39. at the mercy of

〔註〕：形容詞片語，任…之處置，在…之掌握中。

例1. They're at our mercy now.
他們正在我們的掌握之中。

例2. The picnic was at the mercy of the weather.
野餐視天氣而定。

40. at worst

〔註〕：副詞片語，最壞的情況，最壞的打算。

例：When Don was caught cheating in the examination,he thought that at worst he would get a scolding.
當Don考試作弊被逮到，他想最壞情況是被痛責一番。

II. 短句，常用句型練習

※1. It's awesome!

同It's great!

It's wonderful!

〔註〕：太棒了之意。波士頓、新英格蘭地區常用，對感覺，事物等之讚美。awesome指引起敬畏的。

The feeling is awesome.

感覺太棒了。

※2. **It's awful！**

〔註〕：太差勁了，太糟了。指凡是可看到的，聽的或吃的東西等。

例1. The food is awful.

這食物太難吃。

例2. Q：This is their latest hit,how do you like it？

A：It's awful!I don't understand how you can listen to that noise.

問：這是他們最新的熱門歌曲，你喜歡嗎？

答：太爛了！我真不懂你怎麽能聽這麽吵的音樂。

3. **It's amazing！**

〔註〕：太奇妙了，太令人驚異了！每到週末我的錶就停擺

It's amazing！太奇妙了！

※4. **I can't afford it**

〔註〕：我付不起，我買不起。

例：It's too expensive,I can't afford it.

太貴了，我買不起。

※5. **I appreciate your helping me.Thank you so lot.**

我感激你的幫忙，真謝謝了。

PART(B)

Ⅰ. 常用單字，俚語，俗語，非正式用語

1. Boycott

［bɔɪ͵kat］

〔註〕：vt聯合抵制，聯合排貨或絕交。

To boycott the goods of a certain country.

抵制某些國家貨物。

例：They tried to boycott him.

他們企圖和他絕交。

2. Oh, boy!

〔註〕：表驚訝，哦，太棒了。

※3. Buddy

〔註〕：【美俗】指朋友，同伴。電視，電影中常會聽到，常用於較熟悉的朋友稱兄道弟。

例1. Take it easy, buddy.

兄弟，別緊張。

例2. Are you going home, buddy?

老兄，你正要回家嗎？

※4. Baloney

［bəloni］

〔註〕：n.【俚語】胡言，謊言，荒謬的。

例1. It's baloney.

這是個謊言。

例2. Let us cut the baloney on this subject.
我們放棄這荒謬的主題吧。

5. Bear & spirit

〔註〕:啤酒和各種酒類。spirit是酒的意思。這是一些招牌廣告看板,常用吸引顧客的。

6. Blonde [bland] n.

〔註〕:指金黃色頭髮,碧眼和白皙皮膚的女郎。
Blonde girl 金髮美女
Brunett [bru'nɛt] n.則是指髮、膚、眼睛均為褐色之女子。

※7. bucks

〔註〕:【美俗】,等於dollars,如Ten bucks,即Ten dollars,10美元。
美國小額錢幣分one dollar(一塊錢),one quarter(2角5分,即25分),one dime(1角,即10分),one nickle(5分錢),one penny(1分錢)。
須特別注意的是one dime(1角)幣值較one nickle(5分)大,但形狀卻反而小。初抵美國偶會弄迷糊。打pay phone(公共電話)常投入one dime,但有些地方則是投入one quarter。

※8. Bill 賬單,法案,廣告招貼等不同意義

〔註1〕n.當賬單解。到餐廳用完餐結帳時,"waiter, Bill please","侍者,請結帳"。

〔註2〕:法案,議案

例:The bill was introduced into Congress.

這議案已向國會提出。

〔註3〕：指廣告，招貼

例：Post no bills. 請勿張貼。

※9. Bodyguard 保鑣、護衛

['badɪˌgard]

例：He never goes out without a bodyguard.
他沒有保鑣從不外出。

※10.Book

〔註1〕事先預訂機票，房間等

例1. Book hotel room
預訂旅館房間。

2. Have you booked the ticket in advance?
你是否事先訂好機票。

〔註2〕警察逮捕、押解人犯

例：Book him, Murder 1.
一級謀殺罪，把他押起來。

※11. boring

〔註〕：令人厭煩的，無聊的

例：It's boring.

太無聊了。

12. body building

健身運動

13. Boss

〔註〕指老板或頂頭上司，主管。

例：He is my boss.
他是我主管。

14. baby kisser

〔註〕：【俚語】，政治上競選某公職的候選人，為打艮好形象，常在公衆場合親親小孩，以示和藹可親，及充滿愛心。美、蘇高峰會談時前共黨頭子科巴契夫也學會這招，可見人同此心。共產世界也不例外。

例：Nixon was a baby kisser when he ran for vice president with Eisenhower.
當尼克森與艾森豪搭檔競選副總統時，常在公衆場合親小孩以示愛心。

15. back and forth

〔註〕：前後來回的

例1. The chair is rocking back and forth.
這椅子前後搖擺著。

例2. The tiger is pacing back and forth in his cage.
老虎在籠子裡來回走來走去。

※16. back out

〔註1〕：【非正式】用語，指不守信，毀約

例1. He agread to help him with a loan, but backed out.
他同意幫他貸款，但他食言了。

例2. She backed out of her engagement.
她取消她的婚約。

※17. back seat driver

〔註〕：【非正式】用語，指坐在車子後座命令開車者做這，做那的令人討厭傢伙。

例：The man who drove the car became angry

with the back seat driver.

開車的人對討厭嘮叨的後座乘客發脾氣。

※18.**back up**

〔註1〕：移回原位

例：The train was backing up.

火車又開回來了。

※〔註2〕：支持，同意，幫助

例1：The principal backs up the faculty.

校長支持教職員。

例2：Jim has joined the Boy scouts and his father is backing him up.

Jim加入男童子軍，他的父親很支持他。

19. **bail out**

〔註〕：從拘留所，監獄保釋出來，或保釋金

例：When college students got into trouble with the police,the college president would always bail them out.

當大學生給警察惹麻煩時，校長總是把他們保釋出來。

※20. **beat it**

〔註〕：【俚語】很不客氣的口氣叫人滾開，走開之意。電影，電視影集常可聽到，同go away, get out。

例1. The big boy said, “Beat it,kid.We don't want you with us.”

大男孩說，〝滾開，小子，我們不要你同行。〞

例2. When he heard the crash he beat it as fast

as he could.

當他聽到暴裂聲，儘快的跑開了。

21. **beat one's brains out**

〔註〕：動詞片語，【俚語】，指絞盡腦汁，努力去了解。

例：It was too hard for him and he beat his brains out trying to get the answer.

這問題太難了，他絞盡腦汁設法解答。

※22. **Oh,I'm beat**

=I'm tired

〔註〕：我太累了。指精疲力盡。

※23. **beat up**

〔註〕：【非正式】用語，指狠狠的打一頓

例1. I'll beat you up.

我要棒你一頓。

例2. The tough boy said to Bill, "If you come around here again,I'll beat up on you."

兇悍的男生對Bill說，〝如果你再到這裡來，我會好好打你一頓。〞

※24. **you beat me**

你把我難倒了

〔註〕：【非正式】，beat當難倒之意，即你把我問倒了。

同you really got me

例：This problem beats me.

這問題把我難倒了。

25. **beat around the bush**

〔註〕：【俚語】旁敲側擊，說話拐彎抹角，說話繞圈子，顧左右而言他

例1. He beat around the bush for a half hour without coming to the point.
他說話拐彎抹角半個鐘頭，卻一點也沒說到重點。

例2. He would not answer yes or no,but beat around the bush.
他沒回答是否，只是繞圈子。

※26. because of

〔註〕：因為，由於

例：The train arrived late because of the snow storm.
因為大風雪，火車延誤抵達。

27. before long

〔註〕：副詞片語，不久，立刻

例1. Class will be over before long.
不久上課就結束了。

例2. We were tired of waiting and hoped the bus would come before long.
我們等得不耐煩，希望公車不久就來了。

28. behind one's back

〔註〕：副詞片語，背後道人是非不誠懇的。非正人君子所樂為也。

例1. Say it to his face,not behind his back.
當面對他說，不要背後批評人家。

例2. It is not right to criticize a person behind

his back.

背後批評別人是不對的。

29. behind the times

〔註〕：形容詞片語。落伍的，不合時代的，老舊的

例1. Johnson's store is behind the times.

John先生的商店太舊了。

例2. The science books of 30 years ago are behind the times now.

30年前的科學書籍，現在已經落伍了。

※30. Believe it or not

〔註〕：信不信由你。有個電視節目專門介紹一些稀奇古怪，不可思議的人、事、物。

※31. believe one's eyes (or believe one's ear)

〔註〕：動詞片語，確信看到的事物，相信所看到的。有驚訝的感覺。

例1. She saw him there but she could hardly believe her eyes.

她看到他在那裡，但她幾乎不相信她的眼睛。

例2. Is that a plane?

Can I believe my eyes?

那是飛機嗎？我真不敢相信我的眼睛嗎？

例3. Is he really coming? I can hardly believe my ears.

他真的要來嗎？我幾乎不敢相信我的耳朵。

※32. bet one's boots (or bet one's bottom dollar, or bet one'shirt)

〔註1〕：動詞片語，【非正式】用語，指傾其所有與

人打賭。

例：This horse will win.I would bet my bottom dollar on it.

這匹馬一定會贏的，我敢傾所有錢打賭。

〔註2〕：非常肯定的，毫無疑問。

例：Jim said he would bet his boots that he would pass the examination.

Jim說他敢打賭，他一定會通過考試。

※33. big deal

〔註〕：常用口語，【俚語】，【俗語】。重音加強在deal字上。

指瑣碎事，不重要的，不特別的事物。

例1. No big deal （＝Nothing special）沒什麼了不起。

例2. So you become college president.-big deal！所以你當了大學校長，有什麼了不起！！（我才不在乎呢！）

※34. blow up

〔註1〕：破壞，毀滅，爆炸毀滅

例1. He blew up the car by means of a concealed bomb.

他利用隱藏炸彈破壞車子。

例2. The ship blew up.

船爆炸了。

〔註2〕：【非正式】用法，指大發脾氣，失去控制

例：When the secretary asked for the day off, the manager blew up.

當秘書要求放假時，經理大發脾氣。

※35. **bottom line (n.)**

〔註1〕：常用於口語，The essential point，指重要的，最重要部份，重點等意思。

例：The bottom line is how to keep your teeth in good condition.

重要的是如何保持你牙齒的健康。

〔註2〕：最後的結果

※36. **Bottom up !**

〔註〕：【美俗】乾杯，敬酒時把一杯酒喝乾。Cheer！則是「隨意」，高興喝多少就多少。

37. **Both…and**

〔註〕：用於強調談論兩件或更多的事。

例1. Both Frank and Mary were at the party.

Frank和Mary兩人都參加宴會。

例2. Bill is both a good swimmer and a good cook.

Bill是一位好的游泳健將也是一位好的廚師。

38. **Box office**

〔註〕：戲院等之售票室。

※39. **break into**

〔註1〕：V.強行進入，闖入，非法闖入。

例1. Thieves broke into the store at night.

小偷晚上闖入商店。

〔註2〕：【非正式】用語，成功的踏入或開始（事業，生意，社會生活等）。

例1. He broke into television as an actor.

他順利踏入演藝界當演員。

40. break off

〔註1〕：突然的停止

例1. When Bob came in, Jean broke off her talk with Linda and talked to Bob.
當Bob進來時，Jean突然停止和Linda說話而轉向對Bob說話。

※〔註2〕：【非正式】用語，中斷友誼或愛情。

例1. She broke off with her best friend.
她和她最好的朋友鬧翻了。（絕交了）

例2. I hear that Tom and Alice have broken off.
我聽說Tom和Alice分手了。

41. break through

〔註〕：克服克難，突破

例1. Salk failed many times but he finally broke through to find a successful polio vaccine.
沙克失敗好幾次後，最後終於克服困難成功的發明沙克疫苗。

例2. Jim studied very hard this semester in college, and he finally broke through onto the Dean's List for the first time.
Jim這學期非常用功，他終於第一次贏得在系主任優秀名單上。

※42. bring up

〔註〕：養育，扶養長大。照顧，訓練

例1. Joe was born in Texas but brought up in Oklahoma.

Joe在德州出生，但在奧克拉荷瑪長大。

例2. He gave much attention and thought to bringing up his children.

他花費很多心思去養育他的小孩。

※43. brush up

〔註〕：溫習，復習，練習

例1. He brushed up his assignment.

他溫習他的家庭課業。

44. bubble gum music (n.)

〔註〕：【俚語】指搖滾樂（rock'n'roll），為大多數年青未成年（teenagers）所喜歡的音樂，又叫又吼的吵雜音樂。

例：When will you learn to appreciate Mozart instead of that bubble gum music?

什麼時候你才能學會欣賞莫札特音樂，而不是吵雜的搖滾樂。

※45. buckle down

〔註〕：努力，全心全力工作，參與。

例1. You had better buckle down.

你最好努力用功。

例2. Jim was fooling instead of studying;So his father told him to buckle down.

Jim不好好讀書，終日嬉戲，他父親告訴他要努力用功。

46. build up

※〔註1〕：鍛練身體

例：Fred exercised to build up his muscles.

Fred做運動鍛練他的肌肉。

〔註2〕：造成，做成，建造。

例：Lois built up a cake of three Layers.

Lois做了三層厚的蛋糕。

※47. burn out

〔註1〕：動詞片語，被火燒壞或過熱破壞。

例1. Mr. Jones burned out the clutch on his car.

Jones先生燒壞了車子的離合器。

例2. The light bulb in the bathroom burned out, and Father put in a new one.

浴室的燈泡燒壞了，父親裝了一個新的。

〔註2〕：用盡所有的力量。

例：Bill burned himself out in the first part of the race and could not finish the competition.

Bill在徑賽的第一回合就用盡了力氣，以致不能完成比賽。

※48. butter up

〔註〕：【非正式】用語。為常用口語，拍馬屁，討好別人。所謂禮多必詐，對此鼠輩宜多加小心。

※例1. Don't butter me up！（或stop butter me up！）

別拍我馬屁了。

例2. He began to butter up the boss in hope of being given a better job.

為了希望穫得更好的工作，他開始拍老板的馬屁。

49. by chance

〔註〕：副詞片語，偶然地，意外地。

例1. Tom met Bill by chance.

Tom偶然間遇到Bill。

例2. The apple fell by chance on Bobby's head.

蘋果偶然掉到Bobby的頭上。

※50. by means of

〔註〕：當介詞。利用，憑藉著。

例1. The fisherman saved himself by means of a floating log.

漁夫憑藉著飄流的木頭救了他自己。

例2. He made his fortune by means of smuggling.

他靠走私致富。

51. by mistake

〔註〕：誤用，做錯了，錯誤的結果

例1. I used your towel by mistake.

我誤用了你的毛巾。

例2. He picked up the wrong hat by mistake.

他誤拿了別人的帽子。

※52. by no means

〔註〕：決不，同certainly not

例1. He is by no means bright.

他一點也不聰明。

例2. Son: May I stay home from school?

Father: By no means.

兒子：我可以留在家裡不上學嗎？

父親：決不可以。

53. by oneself

〔註〕：副詞片語。獨自地，沒有其他人參與。

例1. Tom liked to go walking by himself.
Tom喜歡獨自去散步。

例2. The house stood by itself on a hill.
這房子孤立在山坡上。

例3. John built a flying model airplane by himself.
John自己做了一架會飛的模型飛機。

※54. by the way

〔註〕：副詞片語，即順便提及，補充說明。常用於當介紹主題時忽然想起的事。

例：We shall expect you;by the way,dinner will be at eight.
我們都期待你；順便一提，晚餐8點開始。

55. by turns

〔註〕：副詞片語，輪流地。

例1. The teachers were on duty by turns.
老師們輪流值勤。

例2. On the drive to Chicago,the three men took the wheel by turns.
開車到芝加哥途中，三位男士輪流開車。

II. 短句，格言，句型練習

※1. You blew it!

你把事情搞砸了！

〔註〕：責怪別人把事情弄得愈糟。

2. Be my guest

同This is my treat
The bill is on me
我請客。
〔註〕：與女朋友約會，用餐畢常必說英語。否則下次約會準泡湯。

※3. **Take a break**
〔註〕：休息一會。工作，讀書後的休息。

4. **I'll be back in a second.**
我馬上回來。
〔註〕：短暫離開

5. **Birds of a feather flock together.**
〔註〕：【格言，proverb】諺語。意同中文的「物以類聚」。
例：Don't be friends with bad boys. People think that birds of a feather flock together.
不要和壞男孩在一起。人家會認為物以類聚。

※6. **Blood is thicker than water.**
〔註〕：【格言】「血濃於水」，表示骨肉親情之強烈感情甚於他人。古今中外皆然。
例：Mr. Jones hires his relatives to work in his store. Blood is thicker than water.
Jones 先生僱用他的親戚在店裡工作，真是血濃於水。

PART(C)

Ⅰ．常用單字，俚語，俗語

1．cab

〔註〕：出租汽車，即Taxi

例：Call a cab for me,please.

請替我叫一輛計程車。

※2．cafeteria

[kæfə'tiriə]

〔註〕：自助餐廳，如學校，附設餐廳。顧客自己動手端盤子選擇自己喜歡的食物，完全自助的方式。

3．call toll free.

〔註〕：免費電話。美國的一些公司行號有些服務電話，只要撥call toll free 1-800-xxxx，即可以免費接通。

4．catch-22

〔註〕：指左右為難。原為一本書名，後來用以比喻左右為難，做也不是，不做也不是。人生當中有很多時候都會遭遇到很難的抉擇。

5．character

['kæriktə]

〔註〕：指文字，記號

例：Chinese character

中國字。

6. chef

〔註〕：廚師

7. comedy

［kə'midiən］

〔註〕：喜劇，滑稽戲。comedian喜劇演員

8. clumsy

〔註〕：笨拙的，笨手笨腳的。例clumsy lady 笨拙的女人

9. congratulation !

〔註〕：恭喜，恭賀之意。祝賀別人金榜題名，或當選之賀詞。

10. creature

［krɪtʃə］

〔註〕：n.動物，animal

例：a lovely creature.

可愛的動物。

※11. certainly not

〔註〕：當然不是。

※12. Come on in

〔註〕：請進。有人在門口按鈴或敲門時回答用語。

13. common sense

〔註〕：普通常識。make sense則是合理的，nonsense 無理的，無意義的。

例：She has no common sense.

她真沒常識。

例：Don't talk nonsense !

不要胡說八道！

14. T.V. commercial

〔註〕：指電視上的商業廣告。Advertisement則是指報紙上的廣告。

※15. cop

〔註〕：【非正式】用語，警察，條子。最常聽到對警察稱呼，電視，電影皆可聽到。
其他常用【俚語】尚有officer，pig，（歹徒最痛恨警察罵其為豬玀），smokey，flatfoot，fuzz，policeman常於書上看上。

例：Cop is coming.
警察來了。

※16. coupon

['kupan]

〔註〕：優待券。美國一些超級市場常用促銷方法，即贈送優待券。

17. credit card

〔註〕：信用卡。美國人習慣使用支票，信用卡付帳，現金交易限於小額交易。使用信用卡購物，平常不覺怎麼樣，到月底結帳，才會令人心疼。

18. cover girl

〔註〕：雜誌上美麗的封面女郎。

※19. call off

〔註〕：取消，停止任何計劃

例1. The baseball game was called off because of rain.
因為下雨，棒球賽取消了。

例2. Let us call off the trip.
讓我們取消旅行計劃。

※20. call up

※〔註1〕：打電話給某人。常用於口語會話

例1. Mark,call me up.（或give me a call）
Mark打電話給我吧。

例2. I'll call you up.
我會打電話給你。

例3. She called up a friend just for a chat.
她打電話給朋友只是為了聊天。

〔註2〕：指法院，律師傳喚證人

例：The district attorney called up three witnesses.律師傳喚參位證人。

〔註3〕：回憶起，使想起

例：The picture of the Capitol called up memories of our class.trip.
美國國會的照片喚起我們班上旅遊的回憶。

21. carry away

〔註〕：使引起強烈的感覺，如太興奮或快樂而失去冷靜的判斷力。深深地影響所感動。

例1. The music carried her away.
音樂使她忘了一切。

例2. He let his anger carry him away.
生氣影響了他的判斷。

22. carry off

〔註〕：勝利，挑戰成功

例1. Bob carried off honors in science.

Bob在科學界贏得榮譽。

例2. Jim carried off two gold medals in the track meet.

Jim在田徑賽中贏得兩面金牌。

※23. carry out

〔註〕：實行，付諸行動，完成。

例1. The generals were determined to carry out their plan to defeat the enemy.

將軍決定把打擊敵人的計劃付之行動。

例2. John listerned carefully and carried out the teachers instruction.

John小心的傾聽，並實踐老師的指示。

※24. To cash a check

〔註〕：以支票向銀行兌現款

例：The bank will cash your ten-dollar check.

銀行將你的十元支票兌付現金。

※25. catch cold

〔註〕：動詞片語，感冒，著涼

一般症狀：

running nose 流鼻涕

sneezing 打噴嚏

sore throat 喉頭痛

fever 發燒

例：Don't get your feet wet, or you'll catch cold.

別把腳弄濕，否則你會感冒的。

26. catch fire

〔註〕：著火

例：When he dropped a match in the leaves, they caught fire.

當他把火柴丟到樹葉，就著火了。

※27. catch on

〔註1〕【非正式】用語，了解，理解，常與to連用。

例1. Don't play any tricks on Joe. When he catch on, he will beat you.

不要向Joe耍詐，當他知道時，他會揍你的。

例2. It's take for a long time for me to catch it on.

我花了很長時間才弄明白。

例3. You'll catch on to the job after you've been here a while.

你在此待一陣子後你會了解這工作的。

〔註2〕：流行，變得普遍

例：The song caught on and was sung and played everywhere.

這首歌變得流行且到處有演唱。

28. catch one's eye

〔註〕：吸引別人的注意，To attract your attention

例：The dress in the window caught her eye when she passed the store.

當她經過商店時，櫥窗的衣服吸引了她。

29. catch sight of

〔註〕：突然見到，偶見。

例：Allan caught sight of a bird in a maple tree.

Allan突然看到一隻鳥在楓樹上。

※30. catch up

〔註1〕：1. 突然接住，2. 抓住某樣東西，3. 拿走

例：She caught up the book from the table and ran out of the room.

她突然從桌上拿起書本跑出室外。

※〔註2〕：趕上，追趕，追隨

例1. You have to work hard in order to catch up with the rest of the class.

為了趕上班上其他同學，你必須要努力用功。

※例2. Q:Do you want to come with me?

A:I catch up.（同I come later. I catch you later.）

問:要跟我一起走嗎？

答:我隨後就到。

〔註3〕：找到，逮捕

例：A man told the police where the robbers were hiding,so the police finally caught up with them.

有人告訴警察搶匪藏匿的地方，警察終於把他們逮捕了。

31. chain-smoke（v）

〔註〕：指抽香煙或雪茄一根接一根不停的抽

例：Mr. Jones is very nervous.He chain-smokes cigars.

Jones先生很緊張，雪茄一根接一根的猛抽。

32. chalk up（v）

〔註〕:【非正式】用語,記錄,記下分數

例:The scorekeeper chalked up one more point for the home team.

記分員替主隊又記錄一分。

33. charge account

〔註〕:記帳。即與商店的一種合約,你可以買東西先使用,後付款。

例1. Mr. Jones has a charge account at the garage on the corner.

Jones先生在轉角的修車廠可先記帳。

例2. Mother bought a new dress on her charge account.

母親利用記帳買了一件新衣。

※34. check in

〔註〕:住進旅館時登記,簽名手續或在機場辦理登機報到手續。

例:The last guests to reach the hotel checked in at 12 o'clock.

最後一批客人在12點時抵達旅館登記。

※35. check it out

〔註〕To look,去查看一下,為常用口語。

※36. check out

〔註〕:與chect in意義正好相反。付完旅館費離開

例:The last guests checked out of their rooms in the morning.

最後一批客人早上結帳退房。

※37. cheer up

〔註〕：1. 振作起來，提起精神。2. 鼓勵

例1. Cheer up ! The worst is over.
振作起來！惡運已過。

例2. The support of the students cheered up the losing team and they played harder and won.
學生的支持鼓勵輸隊，使他們更努力而贏得比賽。

※38. chicken out

〔註〕：動詞片語。膽小畏縮，因害怕而退縮。

例1. I decided to take flying lessons but just before they started I chickened out.
我本來決定修習飛行課程，但就在他們開始時我害怕退縮了。

例2. I used to ride a motorcycle on the highway, but I've chickened out.
我過去習慣在高速公路騎摩托車，但現在我不敢了。

38. chip off the old block

〔註〕：名詞片語。【非正式】用法，類似中文的「有其父必有其子」
chip 是碎片，瑣屑

例：From both his looks and his acts,you could see that he was a chip off the old block.
從他的長相和動作兩方面，你可看出他卻是他父親的兒子。

39. clean up

〔註1〕：淸除，把東西按秩序放置妥當。

例1. She cleaned up the house for her party.
她清除房間準備開舞會。

例2. After the dirty job he cleaned up for supper.
做完髒的工作後，他清洗乾淨準備晚餐。

〔註2〕【俚語】，獲利甚豐，賺了很多錢。

例：Dick cleaned up in the stock market.
Dick在股票市場撈了一票。

※40. clear up

※〔註1〕：天氣轉晴，天氣晴朗，變好

例：The weather cleared up after the storm.
暴風雨過後，天氣轉晴了。

〔註2〕解釋，解答，解決。

例1. The teacher cleared up the harder parts of the story.
老師講解故事最難的部份。

例2. Maybe we can clear up your problem.
也許我們可以解決你的問題。

41. cliffhanger (n.)

〔註〕【俗語】指運動或電影的結局未知，使人有緊張懸疑興奮的感覺。

例：Q:Did you see the Guns of Navarrone?
A:It's a regular cliffhanger.
問:你看了 Guns of Navarrone 的電影嗎？
答:它是部緊張懸疑的電影。

42. climb the wall

〔註1〕：動詞片語，【俚語】，【俗語】爬牆壁簡直是不可能，表示對於較具挑戰性的情況一種

情緒化的反應，像挫折感，緊張或急躁的反應等。

例：By the time I got the letter that I was fired, I was ready to climb the wall.

當我收到被革職的信，我充滿挫折感。

〔註2〕：不感興趣，厭煩而不惜代價急於離開。

例：If the chairman doesn't stop talking, I'll climb the wall.

如果主席再不停止說話，我馬上就離開。

43. close down（※＝shut down）

〔註〕：停止所有工作，完全停止工作。

例1. The factory closed down for Christmas.

工廠停工過聖誕節。

例2. The company shut down the factory for Christmas.

公司關閉工廠過聖誕節。

44. coast is clear

〔註〕：看不見敵人或危險；沒有人看見

例1. When the teacher had disappeared around the corner, John said, "Come on, the coast is clear."

當老師在轉角消失時，John說〝好了，沒人看見我們了。〞

例2. When father stopped the car at the stop sign, Mother said, "The coast is clear on this side."

父親在停車號誌處停車時，母親告訴他〝這邊沒有來車。”

※45. coffee break

〔註〕：喝咖啡休息時間。歐美國家習慣在辦公時間，早上10:30或下午3:00左右讓員工短暫休息喝咖啡，聊天以增加工作效率。

例：The girls in the office take a coffee break in the middle of the morning and the afternoon.
辦公室的女生在早上或下午喝咖啡休息聊天。

※46. Come about

＝To take place
＝happen
＝occur

〔註〕：口語常用。發生

例1. Sometimes it is hard to tell how a quarrel comes about.
有時很難辨別爭吵是怎麼發生的。

例2. When John woke up he was in the hospital but he didn't know how that had come about.
當John在醫院醒來，他不知到底發生什麼事。

47. Come back to earth

〔註〕：回到現實生活，別再做夢，幻想，別傻了。

例：After Jane met the movie star it was hard for her to come back to earth.
Jane遇到電影明星後，很難要她回到現實。

※48. come down with

〔註〕：【非正式】，生病，感染疾病。

例1. We all come down with the mumps.
我們都感染了腮腺炎。

例2. After being out in the rain,George came down with a cold.
雨中外出以後，George感染了感冒。

49. come in handy

〔註〕：動詞片語。【非正式】用法，證明有用，有用的。

例：The French he learned in high school came in handy when he was in the army in france.
當他在法國陸軍服役，他在高中時學的法文證明是有用的。

※50. come on

〔註1〕：【非正式】，常用口語，用於命令句，有「讓我們開始吧！」的意思。即Let's get going. Let's get started.

例："Come on,or we'll be late." said Joe,but Lou still waited.
Joe說〝走吧，否則我們會遲到〞，但Lou還要等。

〔註2〕：【非正式】用法，請求某人做某事，即please do it !

例：Come on Laura,you can tell me.
I won't tell anybody.
Laura告訴我吧，我不會告訴任何人的。

51. come out

〔註1〕：出版

例：The book came out two weeks ago.

這本書兩星期前出版了。

※〔註2〕：結果，完成，結束

例1. How did the story come out?

故事的結局如何？

例2. The game came out as we hoped.

比賽結果如我們所預期。

※52. come to the point

＝get to the point

〔註〕：動詞片語。談重點，進入主題別拐彎抹角。

例1. Henry was giving a lot of history and explanation,but his father asked him to come to the point.

Henry舉了許多歷史背景和說明，但他父親要求他說出重點。

例2. A good newspaper story must come right to the point and save the details for later.

好的新聞題材，必須先敍述重點，然後再細節。

※53. come true

〔註〕：實現，美夢成真。

例1. It was a dream come true when he met the president.

見到總統使他美夢成真。

例2. His hope of living to 100 did not come true.

他希望活到100歲的夢想沒有實現。

※54. come up with

〔註〕：想出，提供，供給，給予

例1. The teacher asked a difficult question,but

finally Ted come up with a good answer.
老師問困難問題，但Ted最後想出一個好的答案。

例2. For years Jones kept coming up with new and good ideas.
多年來Jones一直提出好的新觀念。

55. come up

〔註1〕接近，同come close;approach

例：Christmas is coming up soon.
聖誕節即將來臨了。

〔註2〕：與to連用表相等，等值。

例：The new model car comes up to last years.
這新車型與去年一樣好。

56. control room

〔註〕：控制室，指電視廣播室等有許多按鈕和儀器的房間。

例：While a television program is on the air engineers are at their places in the control room.
當電視節目正播出時，機械師們在控制室各就各位。

※57. control tower

〔註〕：指飛機場的控制塔台，指揮機場飛機的起降。

例：We could see the lights at the control tower as our plane landed during the night.
當我們的飛機在晚上降落時，我們可看見機場控制塔台的燈光。

※58. cool

〔註〕：常用口語，【俚語】同superb, first-rate 好的，瀟灑的，酷的。

例1. He is a cool guy.
他是好人。

例2. He is very cool
他很瀟灑。（酷，帥）

59. cool as a cucumber

〔註〕：形容詞片語，【非正式】用語，cucumber是一種絲瓜，冷靜得像絲瓜，意即指某人非常鎮靜，勇敢，沉重。

例：Bill is a good football quarterback, always cool as a cucumber.
Bill是一位優秀的橄欖球四分後衛，他總是保持冷靜。

※60. cool down

〔註〕：冷靜，冷漠，鎮靜。

例：A heated argument can be settle better if both sides cool down first.
如果雙方冷靜下來，激烈的爭論也會緩和下來。

61. countdown

〔註〕：太空科技方面常用語，即倒數計時，如發射火箭，太空船時。

例：Countdown starts at 23:00 hours tomorrow night and continue for 24 hours.
明晚23:00時開始倒數計時，並繼續24小時。

62. count heads

〔註〕：動詞片語，【非正式】用法，算人數，數人

頭。

例：On the class picnic,we counted heads before we left and when we arrived to be sure that no one get lost.

班上的野餐，出發前和抵達時我們都先數一下人數確定沒有人遺失。

※63. count on

＝depend on

＝Bank on

＝rely on

＝trust

〔註〕：常用口語，依賴，信任。

例1. I'll do it;you know you can count on me.

我會做的，你可相信我。

例2. The company was counting on Brown's making the right decision.

公司依賴Brown做正確的決定。

64. cowboy

〔註〕：本來是指西部牛仔。當【俚語】，【俗語】是指開車吊兒郎噹又開快車以顯示其勇敢的人，類似咱們飆車族。

例：Joe's going to be arrested some day,he is a cowboy on the highway.

Joe在公路上飆車，有一天他會被捕的。

65. crack a joke

〔註〕：動詞片語。【俚語】，說笑話，亂蓋，嗅蓋。

例：The men sat around the stove,smoking and

cracking jokes.

男人圍坐火爐邊，抽煙和說笑話亂蓋。

66. cross one's finger

〔註1〕：動詞片語。美國人常以食指，中指交叉扭在一起表示祝好運，幸運。

例1. Mary crossed her fingers during the race so that Tom would win.

賽跑時Mary兩指交叉祝福，使Tom能贏得比賽。

〔註2〕：【非正式】，同Keep one's fingers crossed表示祝好運。

例：Keep your fingers crossed while I take the test.

當我參加考試時，手指交叉祝我好運吧。

67. cry out

〔註1〕：大聲喊叫，尖叫。同scream；shout

例：The woman in the water cried out "Help！".

掉入水中的婦人大喊，〝救命呀！〞

〔註2〕：用於反對，反抗時的叫喊

例：Many people are crying out against the new rule.

許多人叫喊反對新規則。

※68. culture shock

〔註〕：文化震憾，文化隔閡，由於不同文化背景，生活習慣，思想而產生的震驚。留美期間對美國妞的開放作風，ｘｘｘ級電影之普遍，看得你目瞪口呆。吃慣白米飯老中，每天Pizza,Hamburger，皆足於產生Culture shock。而咱們吃香肉的習慣，老美認為不可思議，這就是文化震憾。

69. curl one's hair

〔註〕：動詞片語。【俚語】毛骨悚然。因害怕，震驚，恐怖而使毛髮矗起。

例：The movie about monsters from another planet curled his hair.

電影中〝外星來的怪物〞，使他看得毛骨悚然。

※70. cut it out

〔註〕：【俚語】，為常用口語，制止別人的揶揄或說風涼話。停止；just stop

※例1. Cut it out（同knock it off）

算了別再說了。

例2. All right,now-Lets cut out the talking.

好了，別再說了。

例3. He was teasing the dog and Joe told him to cut it out.

他正戲弄著狗，Joe叫他停止。

II. 常用短句，格言，句型練習

71. can you handle taht?

你能應付得了嗎？

〔註〕：handle,n.是把手，柄。V.t.指揮，管理。

72. I catch you later.

我隨後找你。

※73. piece of cake

〔註〕【非正式】常用口語，指非常容易；Very

easy；really easy.

另例：That problem is a piece of cake for her,she's an expert in that field.

那問題對她太容易了，她是那方面的專家。

※74. keep the change

〔註〕：零錢不用找了。

75. Children and fools speak the truth.

〔註〕：【格言】諺語，小孩和傻瓜才會說實話。相關中文，即「童言無忌」。

小孩天真無邪，說話往往不加思索。

例：″Uncle Willies is too fat″,said little Agnes. ″Children and fools speak the truth.″ said her father.

小安琪說“Willies舅舅太胖了。”

她爸爸說“童言無忌。”

※76. Could you do me a favor？

同＝Could you give me a hand？

＝May I ask you a favor？

〔註〕：請你幫個忙好嗎？請別人幫忙常用的口語。

※77. I'm crazy about her.

〔註〕：我為她痴迷。

78. She is very cute.

她很可愛。

〔註〕：cute 可愛的。

79. He's clean.

他沒帶武器。

〔註〕：cop攔住嫌疑犯，搜身查驗時，沒有發現歹徒攜帶武器用語。即他沒攜帶武器。

PART(D)

I．常用單字，俚語，俗語

※1. **Delicious 美味的**

［dɪ'liʃəs］

〔註〕：指食物的美味

a delicious meal 佳餚

2. **Democracy**

〔註〕：民主政治，像美國式的民主。

3. **Dictatorship**

〔註〕：獨裁政治，像共產世界

獨裁統治，終為百姓所唾棄。

Dictator 獨裁者。

※4. **Dealer**

〔註〕：經銷商

5. **Decoy** ［dɪ'kɔɪ］

〔註〕：餌，引誘他人使陷於危險的人或物。警方辦案常用於計誘壞人上當。

※6. **Discrimination 種族岐視**

〔註〕：美國法律制定不能有種族岐視，違反者受罰。

7. **Doc 醫師**

〔註〕：Doctor之縮寫。

8. **Dorm**

〔註〕：Dormitory.之縮寫

學校宿舍。

※9. To drop a course

〔註〕：退選一門課程。

※10. due

〔註〕應付的，應到的，預期的。

1. due to由於……而產生

2. on due到期應付的款

例：When is the rent due？

房租應於何時付給？

11. dash off

〔註〕：急寫或急草，特別是指寫或畫

例1. I must dash off a few leters before I go out.

我出門以前必須急速寫幾封信。

例2. Ann took out her drawing pad and pencil and dashed off a sketch of the Indians.

Ann拿出她的畫版和筆快速描繪出印地安人的輪廓。

12. day and night

〔註〕：日以繼夜。連續不斷。

例1. Some filling stations on great highways are open day and night 365 days a year.

在大的高速公路有些加油站是一年365天全天候服務。

例2. The three man took turns driving the truck,and they drove day and night for three days.

三位男士輪流駕駛貨車，連續開了參天參夜。

※13. **daylight saving time（簡寫D.S.T.）**

〔註〕：美國夏令節約時間約從五月開始，比標準時間提前一個小時。

例：Many places in the United States keep their clocks on daylight saving time in the summer.

美國許多地方夏天實施夏令節約時間，把時鐘撥快一小時。

14. **die down**

〔註〕：漸漸停止，或漸漸減弱，變小。

例1. The wind died down.

風漸漸減弱了。

2. The music died away.

音樂聲逐漸消失。

3. His mothers anger died away.

他母親生氣逐漸消了。

15. **die out**

〔註〕：死亡或逐漸消失到完全沒有。

例1. This kind of birb is dying out.

這種鳥漸漸絕跡。

2. If you pour salt water on grass,it dies out.

如果你潑鹽水在草地上，它就枯萎掉了。

※16. **dig in**

※〔註1〕：【非正式】，開始吃吧，用餐吧，在家或餐廳用餐時勸人用餐，即開動吧，吃吧。

例1. Well, dig in!

好，吃飯吧！

2. Mother set the food on the table and told the children to dig in.

母親把食物放在桌上告訴孩子們去吃。

〔註2〕【非正式】，掘壕溝自衛以防敵人攻擊。

例1. The soldiers dug in and waited for the enemy to come.

士兵挖壕溝等待敵人來到。

※17. do out of

〔註〕：【非正式】用法，指使用欺騙手段使蒙受損失。

例：The clerk in the store did me out of ＄2.00 by overcharging me.

店員騙我多算2元美金。

※18. do up

※〔註1〕：常用口語，【俗語】包起來，綁起來。即tie up;wrap

例：Joan asked the clerk to do up her purchases.

Joan要求店員把她買的東西打包起來。

〔註2〕：整理好，收拾好，綁好頭髮，紮好。

例：Do up your hari.It is all loose.

你的頭髮都散了，把它紮好。

〔註3〕：【非正式】用語。穿好衣服。

例1. Do up your coat.

穿好你的外衣。

2. Suzie was done up in her fine new skirt and blouse.

Suzie穿著她的新裙子和襯衣。

※19. do the business

〔註〕：動詞片語。【非正式】用法。指採取適當的反應，做該做的事，做正經事。get the job done

例1. When the little boy cut his finger a bandage did the business.
小男孩割傷了他的手指，繃帶正好派上用場。

2. The boys had trouble in rolling the stone, but four of them did the business.
男孩們搬運石頭有困難，但他們四人卻把石頭搬動了。

※20. double-check

〔註〕：核對兩次，很小心的核對。

例1. When the last typing of his book was finished,the author double-checked it.
當書最後打字完成後，作者詳細核對兩次。

2. The proofreader double checks against errors.
校對者詳細核對兩次避免錯誤。

21. double-cross

〔註〕：黑吃黑，(黑社會份子常耍的手段。)

例：He tried to double cross me.
他想對我黑吃黑。

※22. double date

〔註〕：【非正式】兩對男女一起約會。

例：John and Nancy went with Mary and Bill on a double date.

John和Nancy一起和Mary和Bill兩對出去約會。

美式約會，戀愛到結婚過程相關用語，美國是個崇向自由的國家，關於子女交友，家長都鼓勵其自由交往，約會是最平常的認識異性方法。

①group dating—如聚餐，picnic，party等，可以認識更多的朋友。

②double date—兩對男女一起約會，通常是較正式的，男女雙方都會打扮得「正經八百」，如果頗談得來再個別約會，即single dating個自帶開奮鬥。

例：男：May I have a date with you tomorrow night,Mary.

女：Well I geuss so.

男：明天晚上我可以跟妳約會嗎？

女：嗯，我想可以吧。

③go steady—雙方談得來，繼續單獨和同一人約會，但不表示一定要結婚，只是希望增大。

例：Mary is my date now,I am going steady with her.

Mary是我的女朋友，我和她固定約會。

④engagement—訂婚

⑤wedding shower—結婚前夕，親朋好友都會送禮物給即將結婚新婚夫婦，禮物如雨淋般的多，稱wedding shower。

⑥wedding ceremory—結婚儀式，一般美國家庭都選擇在教堂舉行，在神父祝福下有情人終成眷屬。典禮後會有reception招待會，茶點招待親

友。

23. double park

〔註〕：V.路邊兩車平行停車。雙向停車妨礙交通甚鉅，台北街頭也可常見景像。

例1. Jimmy's father double-parked his car and the police gave him a ticket.

Jimmy的父親違規雙向停車，警察給他開了罰單。

2. If you double—park,you block other cars from passing.

如果雙向停車，你阻礙其他車輛通行。

※24. double play

〔註〕n.棒球術語，棒球迷不可不知，即雙殺出局。

例：The Tigers had a man on first base with one out, but the next batter hit into a double play.

老虎隊一人出局，一壘有人，但下一位打擊手卻擊出一支雙殺出局。

25. draw a line

〔註〕：動詞片語，區別，想出不同。

例1. The law in this country draws a line between murder and manslaughter.

在這國家的法律謀殺和過失殺人是有區別的。

2. Can you draw a line between a lie and a fib?

你能區別說謊與撒小謊有什麼不同嗎？

26. dress up

〔註〕：盛裝，穿最好的或特別的衣服。

例1. Billy hated being dressed up and took off his best suit as soon as he got home from Church.
Billy討厭盛裝，當從教堂回家，他立刻脫掉漂亮衣服。

※27. drop a line

〔註〕動詞片語【非正式】用法，寫信，寄信。

例1. Please drop a line to me when you get to Boston.
當你抵達波士頓時，請寫信給我。

2. Judy's friend asked her to drop her a line while she was way on vacation.
Judy的朋友要她渡假時寫信給她們。

3. Drop me a line when you get there.
當你抵達時，請寫信給我。

※28. drop by (=stop by)

〔註〕：短暫的停留偶訪，順道拜訪。

例1. Drop by any time you're in town.
到城裡來時，歡迎隨時來訪。

2. Don't forget to stop by at the gas station.
別忘了順路到加油站。

3. I've got to drop by the bank to cash a check.
我順道到銀行去兌現支票。

※29. due to (=Beacuse of)

〔註〕：由於……

例：Joe's application to the university was not accepted due to his failing Englinsh.

由於Joe的英文不及格，他申請大學沒有被接受。

※30. drive someone crazy (nuts)

〔註〕：【俚語】，【俗語】常用口語，使某人發狂，迷惑。

聯考的壓力常使人發狂。

例：You're driving me crazy with that kind of talk.

你那樣的說話真使我發狂。

II．短句，格言，句型練習

31. I do

〔註〕：我願意。像電影上常見結婚畫面，牧師問新娘願不願嫁給新郎的回答。Do的用法，口語中很常用，應特別注意。

例1. Q:Oh,I hate to wait like that,you know.

A:I do too.

問:哦，我討厭那樣等待。

答:我也一樣。

例2. You don't like it,do you？

你不喜歡它，是嗎？

※32. I did it (＝I made it)

〔註〕：我做成功了。歡呼表示做成功了。常用口語。同succed

例：David did it.

David made it.

大衛做到了，做成功了。

※33. This brand new T.V. set is dead.

這台嶄新電視機完全壞了。

〔註〕：dead指凡電視，電話或其他電器用品，完全壞了不能再使用。

例：Is this telephone dead?

這電話壞了嗎？

※34. Do you know what I mean?

你明白我的意思嗎？

〔註〕：對別人了解你的意思有懷疑時問語。

35. Did you see what I saw?

看到我所看到的東西嗎？

〔註〕：明明有部車子停在這裡，一會兒不見了，活見鬼。

Did you see what I saw?

36. Don't tourture yourself.

別再折磨你自己了（想開一點吧！）

〔註〕：當看到別人失戀，或失意時，一付自艾自怨自嘆命苦時，趕緊規勸，這又何必呢，天涯何處無荒草，想開一點。

37. Don't push me to hard.

別逼人太甚。

〔註〕：得饒人處且饒人，所謂逼虎傷人。

38. Don't get confused.

別再弄迷糊了。

〔註〕：confused，使混亂，迷惑。

※39. Don't do this to me again.

不要在對我這樣。

〔註〕：不滿別人一再對你惡作劇或不禮貌行為時，告誡用語。

40. Don't peek

〔註〕：別偷看。不滿別人鬼鬼祟祟的偷窺。

※41. Don't buggine me!

＝Don't bother me

＝Don't annoyl me

〔註〕：bug（v.）【俚語】To bother;annoy。別煩我。對別人的喋喋不休表示反感。

42. Don't let me down.

〔註〕：別讓我失望。對別人寄以厚望。

43. Do you eat yet?

〔註〕：吃過飯沒有。看Jenny坐在原位艮久，關切詢問是否吃過中飯沒。

44. Do you wear contact lenses?

你是否戴隱形眼鏡？

〔註〕：contact lenses是指隱形眼鏡。

glasses是眼鏡。在美國，到監理所申請駕照，駕駛人除了須通過口試（oral test）和路試（road test）外，體檢時體檢官可能還會問的句子。

45. It's a deal

一言為定。

〔註〕：對別人達成某程度的約定。

46. Don't worry,everything will be O.K.

別擔心，一切問題都會解決的。

〔註〕：安慰別人不用擔心用語。

47. Yor've dropped something.

你掉了東西。

〔註〕：看到別人掉了東西，提醒其注意。

48. Do you want to dedicate this song to someone?

你要把這首歌獻給某人嗎？

〔註〕：電台廣播節目常會聽到的話。dedicate是奉獻，獻給之意。

2-4 PART(E)

I • 常用單字，俚語，俗語

1. easy going

開朗，樂天派，容易相處的

2. Employer [ɪ'mplɔiə] n.雇主，主人

Employee [ɪmplɔ'i] n.受雇員工，職員

〔註〕：Employee職員，受雇員工，須特別注意發音，重音在ee。

3. Embarrassing

[ɪm'bærəsɪŋ]

令人困窘的，使人難堪的。

〔註〕：女人最忌諱別人問年齡，婚姻，三圍。

Don't ask such embarrassing questions。

不要問這類使人難堪的問題。以免自討沒趣。

※4. Exactly！

完全正確！（對極了！）

〔註〕：常用口語，對別人的看法表示完全同意。就是那麼一回事。

例：That's exactly what I want.

那正是我想要的。

5. exaggerate

[ig'zædʒəret] v.

誇張，誇大

〔註〕：誇大事實。To exaggerate an illness誇大

疾病。

6. Entrance入口

Exit出口

〔註〕：公共場所如戲院，歌劇院等的出入口。

※7. Easy come,easy go.

來的容易，去的也容易。

〔註〕：【非正式】用法。不法錢財來得容易，去的也快，像六合彩，大家樂等。

8. eat out

〔註〕：到外面餐廳用餐。不是在家裡。

例：Tom ate out often even when he wasn't out of town.

Tom甚至沒有出差時也常到外面餐廳用餐。

9. eat and run

〔註〕：指吃完飯就走。與朋友事先有約，結果吃完飯急忙就走，這是很不禮貌。

10. eat up

〔註〕：把東西吃光；食盡。

例1. Eat it up.

把它吃光罷。

2. After hiking all afternoon,they quickly ate up all of the dinner.

遠足一下午，他們很快地吃完所有晚餐的食物。

11. end up

〔註〕：結束，結尾，停止。同finish up

例1. How does the story end up?

這故事是怎麼結尾的？

2. The professor finally ended up his speech.
教授終於結束他的演講。

※12. enjoy of oneself

〔註〕：動詞片語。好好享受，使……快樂。

例1. Mary enjoyed herself at the party.
Mary在宴會上玩得很快樂。

2. "Enjoy yourselves, Children", Mother urged the guests at our party.
母親鼓勵參加我們宴會的小客人說，"孩子們，好好玩呀！"

※13. Excuse me

[ɪk'skjuz]

〔註〕：請教別人客套語，對不起，每天必說，舉凡，問路，借過，請求原諒等。

例：Excuse me a minute!
對不起失陪一下！

14. Extracurricular activity

〔註〕：指學校的課外活動。

II. 短句，格言，句型練習

15. He's a walking encyclopedia

他是一本活的百科全書。
（他是萬能先生，無所不知）

〔註〕：encyclopedia百科全書。此指某人學富五車。

※16. Early bird catches the worm

〔註〕：【格言】。早起的鳥兒有蟲吃，比喻做任何事愈早愈好，成功的機會愈大。但有人偏要

說早起的蟲兒被鳥吃，那未免太悲觀，無可救藥。

例1. Charles began looking for a summer job in January; he knows that the early bird catches the worm.
元月份查理就開始找暑期工作；他懂得「早起的鳥兒有蟲吃」的格言。

2. When Billy's father woke him up for school he said, "The early bird catches the worm."
Billy的爸爸叫醒他去上學時，說"早起的鳥兒有蟲吃"。

17. eye for an eye and a tooth for a tooth

〔註〕：以眼還眼，以牙還牙，來自舊約聖經。怨怨相報，何時了，奉勸各位應化干戈為玉帛。

PART(F)

Ⅰ. 常用單字，俚語，俗語

※1. Fantastic！
太奇妙了！太妙了！
〔註〕：【非正式】superb（美妙的）;wonderful（太棒了）

2. Feed back
〔註〕：迴饋。對於過程結果的反應，回應。特別是改正或控制。

3. front desk
詢問台，服務台
〔註〕：大公司門口的服務台，Receptionst接待員。

4. Frustrate
挫折
〔註〕：學了多年英語，卻無法開口說英語，挫折感可想而知。

※5. flea maket
跳蚤市場
〔註〕：美國有許多市集專賣二手貨，舊貨像古董，傢俱等，價格便宜。台灣也逐漸有舉辦類似的活動。
例：There are many outdoor flea maket in the United States.
美國有許多室外的跳蚤市場。

6. French fry（＝French fried potato）

炸薯條，美式速食餐像麥當勞漢堡餐常吃的炸薯條。

例：Mike ordered a hamburger and french fries.

Mike點了一客漢堡和炸薯條。

7. first—run

〔註〕：形容詞片語。指首輪影片或新的，首映的。

例：The local theater showed only first-run movies.

本地戲院只上映首輪影片。

※8. fix

〔註〕：常用動詞。repair，修理。

例：He can drive,but he knows so little about the car that he can't fix it if anything goes wrong.

他會開車，但對車了解不多，所以一出差錯他不會修理。

※9. Face-to-Face

〔註〕：副詞片語。面對面地，面對的。

例1. I have heard about him,but I never met him face-to-face.

我聽了好多關於他的事，但未曾謀過面。

2. The British Prime minister came to Washington for.a face-to-face meetig with the President.

英國首相到華盛頓與美國總統舉行面對面的會談。

3. The church and the school stand face-to-face across the street.

教堂和學校隔著街對立著。

※10. face up to

〔註〕：面對現實，縱使是困難的或不愉快的事。人生不如意事十常八九，應勇敢的面對挑戰，得意事來處之以淡，失意事來處之以忍。

例：We must face up to our responsbilities and not try to get out of them.

我們必須面對我們的責任，而不要試著去逃避它。

11. fair-weather friend.（n.）

〔註〕：指勢力眼或酒肉朋友，只有當你成功時才是朋友。所謂錦上添花，而不是雪中送炭的朋友。

例：Everyone knows that John's only a fair-weather friend.

大家都知道John是勢力眼的朋友。

12. fall behind（v.）

〔註〕：比別人慢而且落後很多。

例1. John's lessons were too hard for him, and he soon fell behind the rest of the class.

功課對John太難了，不久他比班上同學落後很多。

2. Mary was not promoted because she dreamed too much and fell behind in her lessons.

Mary空想太多，功課卻落後，所以沒有升級。

※13. fall for

〔註1〕：**【俚語】**，開始非常喜歡某事。

例：Dick fell for baseball when he was a little

boy.

當Dick還是小男生時，就開始喜愛棒球。

〔註2〕：開始喜歡，愛上。

例：Helen was a very pretty girl and people were not surprised that Bill fell for her.

Helen是個漂亮小女孩，Bill喜歡她沒有人會感到驚訝。

※14. fall in love

〔註〕：墜入愛河，與（某人）開始戀愛。

例：Tom fell in love with Mary.

Tom和Mary開始戀愛。

※注意Make love to則是指與某人做愛，有性行為關係。

例：It is rumored that Dick makes love to every girl he hires as secretary.

謠傳Dick和每一位他雇用的秘書做愛。

15. fall short（v.）

〔註〕：沒有達到目標，沒有做成功。

例1. His jump fell three inches short of the world record.

他的跳高比世界記錄少3英吋。

2. The movies fell short of expectations.

這部電影沒有預期的好。

※16. fall through（v.）

〔註〕：**【非正式】**，To fail；失敗；沒有去做或實現。

例1. Jim's plan to go to college fell through at

the last moment.

Jim想上大學的計劃，最後沒有實現。

2. Mr. Jone's deal to sell his house fell through.

Jone先生賣房子的交易吹了。

17. fast buck（＝quick buck）

〔註〕：【俚語】橫財，指賺的快而容易的錢財，常是不正當得來的。所謂人無橫財不富，每個人都想一夕致富，大家樂，六合彩盛行，股票狂飆可見。

例：He isn't interested in a career; he's just looking for a fast buck.

他不熱心事業，只想發橫財。

※18. fed up

〔註〕：【非正式】，【俚語】。忍受夠了，討厭，厭煩，疲倦。

例1. I'm fed up.

我受夠了。（不滿別人的抱怨，嘮叨）

2. I'm fed up with your grumbling!

我真受夠了你的嘮叨怨言。（I've had enough of his complaints）

3. People get fed up with anyone who brags all the time.

人們討厭時常喜歡自誇的人。

※19. feel like

〔註〕：【非正式】，很想做……

例：I don't feel like running today.

今天我不想跑步。

※20. feel no pain

〔註〕：動詞片語。【俚語】，失去知覺，像酗酒，醉酒。

例：After a few drinks,the man felt no pain and began to act foolishly.
喝了幾杯以後，這位男士就醉得迷迷糊糊，笨手笨腳。

21. few and far between

〔註〕：形容詞片語，不很多，很稀少，不常見到或發現的。

例1. Places where you can get water are few and far between in the desert.
沙漠中可以取到水的地方很少。

2. Really exciting games are few and far between.
真正令人興奮的比賽太少了。

※22 fifty—fifty

〔註〕：【非正式】用語。常用口語，平分之意，各擁有一半，一半機會。

例1. There is only a fifty-fifty chance that we will win the game.
我們只有一半贏得比賽的機會。

2. When Dick and Sam bought an old car, they divided the cost fifty-fifty.
Dick和Sam合買一部老爺車，他們各自付一半的錢。

23. figure on

〔註〕：當計劃某事時，期望或想像。

例1. He figured on going to town the next day.
他計劃明天到鎮上去。

2. We did not figure on having so many people at the picnic.
我們沒想到會有這麼多人來參加野餐。

※24. figure out

〔註〕：常用於口語，必記。想出，找出答案，發現問題，明白或了解之意。

例1. I can't figure out what's going on.
我想不出到底是怎麽回事。

2. Tom couldn't figure out the last problem on the arithmetic test.
Tom無法想出算術試題最後問題的答案。

3. Sam couldn't figure out how to print a program until the teacher showed him how.
Sam不知道如何印出程式，直到老師教他。

※25. fill in

〔註1〕：填滿空表格。入境他國須填表格，註册時亦須填表格。

例1. You should fill in all the blanks on an application for a job.
你應該把工作申請表格所有空欄填滿。

〔註2〕：取代某人位置，填補。

例：The teacher was sick and Miss Jones filled in for her.

老師生病，Jone小姐代替她上課。

※26. find fault

〔註〕：動詞片語。專找別人毛病，挑剔，批評，找渣。

例1. She tries to please him,but he always finds fault.

她試著去討好他，可是他卻時常挑剔。

2. They found fault with every box I made.

他們挑剔我做的每一個盒子。

※27. find out

〔註〕：發現某事，找出以前不知道的事實。

例1. Mary was angry when Jane found out her secret.

當Jane發現Mary的秘密時，她很生氣。

2. I don't know how this car works,but I'll soon find out.

我不了解這車子怎麼運轉，但不久我就找出原因。

※28. first come,first served

〔註〕：【非正式】用語。按先後順序，先到者，優先被服務。

例1. Get in line for.your ice cream,boys. First come,first served.

喂，孩子們排隊拿冰淇淋，按先後順序。

2. The rule in the restaurant is first come, first served.

飯店的規矩是按優先順序服務。

※29. Follow up

〔註1〕：動詞片語。【非正式】常用語，追蹤考核，緊追不捨，不願放棄。

例：The Indians followed up the wounded bufflalo until it fell dead.

印地安人追蹤受傷的水牛，直到牠倒下死亡。

〔註2〕：追蹤，再加強，使某事做的更完美。

例：The doctor followed up Billy's operation with X-rays and special exercises to make his foot stronger.

醫師利用X光和特別運動追蹤加強Billy的手術，使他的腳更強壯。

※30. fool around（或play around）

〔註〕：【非正式】用語。浪費時間，嬉戲。

例1. If you go to college,you must work,not fool around.

如果你上大學要努力用功，不要荒廢時間。

2. The boys fooled around all afternoon in the park.

男孩子們整個下午在公園嬉戲。

※31. for example（或for instance）

〔註〕：副詞片語。常用於舉例說明，例如……

例1. Not only rich men become President. For example,Lincoln was born poor.

不只有錢人可當總統，例如林肯出生寒微也一樣可當總統。

2. There are jobs more dangerous than truck driving;for instance,training lions.

許多工作比開貨車更危險；例如，訓練獅子。

32. foul ball

〔註〕：棒球術語，棒球迷不可不知，即界外球，犯規的球。

例：Mickey hit a long foul ball that landed on the roof.

Mickey擊出一記降落屋頂的長界外球。

※33. foul up

〔註1〕：【非正式】用語。make a mistake。弄錯，弄混了。

例1. Blue suit and brown socks！He had fouled up again.

穿藍色襯衫和棕色襪子！他又弄混了。

〔註2〕：go wrong。做錯事。

例：Why do some people foul up and become criminals.

為什麼有些人要做錯事而犯法。

34. from Missouri

〔註〕：【俚語】，懷疑，不相信。

例：Don't try to fool me.I'm from Missouri.

別騙我，我不相信你所說的。

II. 常用短句

35. I am full

我吃飽了。

〔註〕：吃很飽撐不下了。

相反則是

I am starving
=I am very hungry
=I can eat a horse

〔註〕：我很餓。我餓扁了。

36. It's not my fault.

這不是我的錯

〔註〕：推卸責任的最佳藉口。公家機關互踢皮球最佳藉口，勿必學會這句。

※37. Forget it

〔註〕：1. 算了吧。對別人的道謝，表示不在意。算了，沒什麼之意。
2. 算不了什麼。

PART(G)

Ⅰ. 常用單字，俚語，俗語

1. gay

男同性戀者

〔註〕：美國是同性戀者的天空，不僅可以公開遊行，甚至上電視現身說法。國內尺度也漸開放，可以談了。上帝造物有時也瘋狂，對同性戀是否應寄予同情見人見智。Lesbian則是指女同性戀者。

※2. guy

〔註〕：人，某某人，傢伙。須特別注意guy與gay字不同，讀音也不同。

※例1. He is a decent guy.
他是大好人。

2. He is a lousy guy.
他是個差勁的人。

※3. Gee !

〔註〕：感嘆詞。【非正式】常用語，老美談話中常可聽到，表示驚訝或其他強烈感覺，少見於正式書寫英語。

例1. Gee ! I am late again.
啊糟啦！我又遲到了。

2. Oh ! Gee ! I forgot my I.D.
啊，糟了！我忘了帶身份證件。

※4. Oh,great!

〔註〕:哦,太棒了。太好了,好極了,太棒了。

例1. That's great!

那太棒了!

2. You sound great.

你真行,你太棒了。

※5. generation gap

〔註〕:【俗語】。指代溝,由於上,下兩代的思想,社會價值,態度,生活形態不同所產生的對抗。新新人類又有不同的價值觀。

例1. My son is twenty and I am forty,but we have no generation gap in our family.

我兒子20歲,而我40歲,但在我們家卻沒有代溝存在。

6. Go!Go!

加油!加油!

〔註〕:拉拉隊常用為隊友打氣。

※7. Go ahead!

〔註〕:常用口語,必記。請便,先請之意。

例1. You go ahead.

你先請吧。

2. Q:May I ask you a question?

A:Go ahead.

問:我可以請教你問題嗎?

答:請便。(請說)

※8. Go on

〔註〕:繼續,不要停。常用口語

例：Go on！I'm listening.
　　繼續說吧！我正傾聽著。

9. garbage down

〔註〕：動詞片語。【俚語】。狼吞虎嚥，饞相。

例：The children garbaged down their food.
　　孩子們狼吞虎嚥。

※10. gas up（或fill up）

〔註〕：【非正式】用語，指替車子或飛機加滿汽油。

例1. The mechanics gassed up the planes for their long trip.
　　機械師替飛機加滿汽油做長途飛行。

2. The big truck stopped at the gas station and gassed up.
　　大卡車停在加油站並加滿汽油。

11. get across

〔註〕：當動詞。清楚地解釋，澄清某事。

例1. Mr. Brown is a good coach beacuse he can get across the plays.
　　Brown先生是一位好教練，因為他解釋比賽容易了解。

2. The teacher tried to explain the problem, but explain did not get across to the class.
　　老師試著解答問題，但學生仍沒弄清楚。

12. get ahead

〔註〕：【非正式】用語。使成功的，有成就的

例1. Mr. Bob was a good Lawyer and soon began to get ahead.

Bob先生是位好的律師，不久他成功了。

2. The person with a good education finds it easier to get ahead.

受良好教育的人發現比較容易成功。

13. get a load of (＝take a good look at)

〔註〕：動詞片語，【俚語】好好的看一眼，指看比較不平常或有趣的。

例1. Get a load of that pretty girl !

看那女孩多正典！

2. Get a load of Dick's new car !

好好看一下Dick的新車！

※14. get along

〔註1〕：友善的相處；同意；合作。

例1. Jim and Jane get along fine together.

Jim和Jane相處得很好。

2. Don't be hard to get along with.

不要太勉強同意。

〔註2〕：同make progress；進步；前進。

例：John is getting along well in school. He is learning more every day.

John在學校功課進步很快，他每天學很多。

15. get a fix on

〔註〕：動詞片語。【俗語】鎖定目標，pilot常用語如以雷達或聲納等電子儀器接收到遠距離的目標。

例：Can you get a fix on the submarine?

你能以電子儀器鎖定潛艇的位置嗎？

※16. get a move on

〔註〕：快點，To hurry up；get going之意。【非正式】用語，【俚語】
當動詞片語，常用於命令口語。必記。

例：Get a move on,or you will be late.
快點，否則你要遲到了。

17. get behind

〔註1〕：進度太慢，落後。

例：The post office get behind in delivering Chrismas mail.
郵局在運送聖誕郵件進度太慢。

〔註2〕：【非正式】用語時，指支持，幫助。

例：We got behind Mary to be class president.
我們支持Mary當班代表。

18. get cracking

〔註〕：動詞片語，【俚語】，【俗語】，與hurry up；get going意同，大部份用於命令語句。

例1. Come on,you guys,let's get cracking!
喂各位，請快點呀！

2. Let's get going.It's almost supper time.
快走呀，晚餐時間快到了。

19. get down to

〔註〕：【非正式】用語，即To get started on；開始工作。

例1. Let's get down to work.
我們開始工作吧。

2. Joe wasted a lot of time before he got down to work.

開始工作前，Joe浪費太多時間。

※20. **get lost**

〔註〕：動詞片語，【俚語】，滾開，走開。常用於命令句。類似用語，Beat it；go away。

例：Get lost！I want to study.

滾開！我要讀書。

※21. **get even**

〔註〕：【非正式】用語，get revenge，報復。君子報仇三年不晚。

例：Last April First Mr. Harris got fooled by Joe, and this year he will get even.

去年四月Joe首先作弄Harris先生，今年Harris先生準備報復。

※22. **come on, get in**

〔註〕：快點，坐進去吧。催促別人坐進計程車，汽車內等。

※23. **get off**

〔註〕：指下車或走下階梯等。

例1. The bus stopped, the door opened, and I got off.

公車停下，打開車門，我就下車了。

2. The ladder fell, and Tom couldn't get off the roof. 梯子倒下，所以Tom不能從屋頂上走下來。

※24. **get off one's back**

〔註〕：動詞片語。【俚語】，【俗語】。電視影集常可聽到，阻止別人的嘮叨不休，不耐煩。滾開別不識相。

例1. Get off my back! Can't you see how busy I am?
滾開別煩我！你沒看到我有多忙呀？

2. I warn you,get off my back.
我警告你，滾開，別再煩我。

25. get one's feet wet

〔註〕：動詞片語，【非正式】用語。弄濕你的腳，意指初次嘗試某事。常用於命令。

例：" It's not hard to dance once you get your feet wet." said the teacher.
老師說："一旦你開始嘗試跳舞並不難。"

※26. get out of my face (or stay out of my way)

〔註〕：走開，滾開。厭惡別人的嘮叨或生氣，不想再看到，見到。

27. get the feel of

〔註〕：動詞片語，使變成習慣或學習，特別是以感覺或手操作，習慣成自然。

例1. You'll get the feel of the job after you've been there a few weeks.
你在那裡幾個星期後，將熟悉你的工作。

2. John had never driven a big car,and it took a while for him to get the feel of it.
John未曾開過大車子，他花了一些時間學習後就習慣了。

28. get the jump on

〔註〕：動詞片語，【俚語】，領先別人，比別人先開始。

例：Don't let the other boys get the jump on you at the beginning of the race.
比賽開始時，別讓其他的男孩領先你。

※29. get the picture

〔註〕：picture是照片，與照片一模一樣，即完全明白之意，完全了解。常用於口語。

例：A:Did you get the picture?
你是否明瞭了嗎？
B:Yes,I got the picture.
是的，我完全明白。

30. get to the bottom of

〔註〕：動詞片語。意指追根究底，發現真正的原因，發現真象。

例1. The doctor made several tests to get to the bottom of the man's headaches.
醫師做了幾個試驗來找出這個人頭痛的原因。

2. The superintendent talked with several students to get to the bottom of the trouble.
督學與數位學生討論以便找出麻煩所在。

※31. get to the point（或come to the point）

〔註〕：動詞片語。有話直說，談論重點別拐彎摸角，開門見山的。

I've get your point 或I see your point.

我明白你的意思。

例1. Joy,get to the point.

Joy有話直說別拐彎摸角了。

2. A good newspaper story must get right to the point and save the details for later.

好的新聞題材必須精要，細節後面再說明。

※32. get up

〔註1〕：起床，

例：It's time to get up.

該是起床的時間了。

〔註2〕：同stand up，起立；站起來。

例：A man should get up when a woman comes into the room.

當女士進入房間時，男士應該起立。

※33. give a hand

〔註〕：常用口語，動詞片語。幫忙，給予某人幫助，伸出援手。

例1. Could you give me a hand with these packages？

請幫我提一下這些行李好嗎？

2. Bob saw a woman with a flat tire and offered to give her a hand with it.

Bob看見一位女士輪胎破了，主動去幫忙。

※34. give a hard time

〔註〕：動詞片語。【非正式】用語，hard time是指困難時刻。當你做某事或談某事時，別人給予找麻煩，刁難之意。

例1. Don't give me a hard time, Dick.
I'm doing my best on this job.
Dick別找我麻煩，我正盡力把工作做好。

2. Jane gave her mother a hard time on the bus by fighting with her sister and screaming.
Jane在公車上和她妹妹打架並尖叫著給她媽媽難堪。

※35. give a pain

〔註〕：動詞片語。【俚語】。常用口語，給予難堪，痛苦，苦惱，厭惡等。

例1. Ann's laziness give her mother a pain.
Ann的懶惰給她母親很難過。

2. Bob's bad manners give his teacher a pain.
Bob惡劣態度給老師很難堪。

36. give in

〔註〕：妥協，同意某人的做法，停止對抗，爭論或打鬥。

例1. After Billy proved that he could ride a bicycle safely, his father gave in to him and bought him one.
Bill證明他會安全地騎腳踏車，他父親同意買一部給他。

2. Mother kept inviting Mrs. Smith to stay for lunch, and finally she gave in.
母親力邀Smith太太午餐，最後她才同意。

※37. give up

〔註1〕：投降，放棄嘗試某事。

例1. The dog had the ball in his mouth and couldn't give it up.
這隻狗口裡含著球，而不願放棄。

2. Never give up
永不放棄。

〔註2〕：停止，放棄等待或繼續做某事。

例1. The doctor told Mr. Harris to give up smoking.
醫師告訴Harris先生停止抽菸。

2. I couldn't do the puzzle so I gave it up.
我猜不出謎題，所以放棄了。

※38. go all the way with

〔註〕：表完全同意，完全滿意。

例1. I go all the way with what George says about Bill.
我完全同意George所說有關Bill的事。

2. Mary said she was willing to kiss Bill, but that did not mean she was willing to go all the way with him.
Mary說她想吻Bill，但那並不表示她完全滿意他。

※39. go Dutch

〔註〕：動詞片語。【非正式】用語。與朋友到餐廳用餐時各自付帳用語。男女約會時國內似乎不流行各自付帳，一律由男士付帳，以表示誠意，才有面子，否則被視為小氣，下次的

約會也會泡湯。

例1. Sometimes boys and girls go Dutch on dates.
有時候男孩和女孩約會也是各自付帳。

2. The girl knew her boy friend had little money, so she offered to go Dutch.
這女孩知道她男朋友沒多少錢，所以提議各自付帳。

※40. go for it

〔註1〕：動詞片語。【非正式】用語。To try to get；try for；try it out；do it 試著去獲得，去做吧，盡力；盡全力做好。為常用口語，必記。go for it

例1. Q:I want to buy a car.
A:Go for it.（＝Buy it）
問:我要買部車子。
答:去買吧。

2. Our team is going for the championship in the game tonight.
晚上的比賽我隊設法要贏得冠軍。

〔註2〕：喜好或支持，喜歡。

例：Little Susie really goes for ice cream.
小Susie非常喜歡冰淇淋。

41. go in one ear and out the other

〔註〕：動詞片語，【非正式】用語，從左邊耳朵聽進，從右邊耳朵出來，表示不專心，不注意聽，把它當耳邊風不當一回事。

例1. Mother scolded Martha,but it went in one ear and out the other.

母親責備Martha，但他只當耳邊風。(Martha一點都不在乎。)

2. The teacher's directions to the boy went in one ear and out the other.

男生把老師的指示當耳邊風。

※42. good looking

〔註〕：面貌姣好，帥哥，酷哥，handsome。

例：John is a good looking guy.

John是位帥哥。

43. go off

〔註1〕：鈴聲，警鈴聲，開始響。

例1. Alarm goes off.

警鈴開始響了。

2. The alarm clock went off at six o'clock and woke Father.

鬧鐘六點開始響，把父親吵醒。

〔註2〕：爆炸。

例：The firecracker went off and scared Jacks dog.

爆竹爆炸嚇壞了Jack的狗。

※44. go steady

〔註〕：動詞片語。只固定與一人約會。即與固定的一位男友或女友繼續約會交往。

例1. Jean went steady with Bob for a year.

Jean和Bob固定約會交往一年了。

2. At first Tom and Mary were not serious about each other,but now they are going steady.
開始時Tom和Mary彼此並不很認真，但現在他們已固定約會交往了。

※45. grow up

〔註1〕：長大，成長，身高或年齡增大。

例1. I grew up on a farm.
我在農村長大。

2. Jack is growing up;his shoes are too small for him.
Jack逐漸長大；他的鞋子已經太小了。

〔註2〕：指心智的成熟

例：Grow up,you're not a bady any more.
該長大了，你不再是小孩子了。（勸別人別再孩子氣了）

II. 常用短句，格言，諺語

※46. God bless you.

願上帝保佑你

〔註〕：1.上教堂最常聽到祝福的話
2.美國人當聽到別人打噴嚏時，亦常如此回答。

※47. I gotcha

〔註1〕：我知道了，我明白了。

〔註2〕：為難，愚弄。即I got you.我把你難倒了。

48. That's gorgeous！那太美了！

〔註〕：gorgeous【俚語】華麗的，爽快的。

例：London is a gorgeous city.From here you can see the palace guards.

倫敦是很高貴的城市，從這裡你可以看到皇宮的侍衛。

49. gone with the wind

〔註〕：形容詞片語【格言】，隨風飄去，表示消失，永別。40或50年代著名電影，由費雯麗和克拉克蓋博主演的不朽名片中譯「亂世佳人」的片名即"Gone with the wind."

例1. All the Indians who used to live here are gone with the wind.

曾經住這裡的所有印地安人已不見了。

2. Joe knew that his chance to get an"A"was gone with wind when he saw how hard the test was.

Joe看到考試是如此難，他知道得A是沒有希望了。

※50. Come on,give me a break.(gimme a break)

〔註〕：常用口語，必記。算了，饒了我吧，別拿我開玩笑了，或別惹我了。制止別人的揶揄或說風涼話。

※51. get the job done

〔註〕：做好須要做的事，即把事情做好。

PART（H）

Ⅰ．常用單字，俚語，俗語，非正式用語

※1. Handout

〔註〕：【非正式】用語，教授，講師上課時所發的講義。

※2. hanky-panky

[hæŋki'pækɪ]

〔註〕【俗語】指做事鬼鬼祟祟或如上司與女秘書等有曖昧關係。

例1. No hanky-panky.
別耍詐。

2. Don't play hanky-panky with me.
別向我耍詐。

3. Hijack

['haidʒæk]

〔註〕【非正式】搶劫或劫機。恐怖份子常幹的勾當。

4. Highlight

〔註〕：重要的事件或細節。

※5. hooker

〔註〕：【俚語】妓女，即prostitute；whore。電視，電影集，警匪片常可聽到。英國名演員休葛蘭，因在洛城找hooker而聲名大躁。

※6. hot dog

〔註〕：熱狗，即麵包夾香腸。

例：The boys stopped on the way home for hot dogs and coffee.

男孩子們在回家途中停下來吃熱狗和喝咖啡。

7. hot potato

〔註〕：【非正式】用語，即中文的燙手山竽，指難以解決的問題。

例：That subject is a hot potato.

那主題是燙手山竽。

8. Happy ending

〔註〕：圓滿的結局，如電視劇「悲歡歲月」以喜劇收場，皆大歡喜。

※9. hot

※〔註1〕：這麽簡單的字，卻有許多不同用法。當熱情的。

例：She is hot.

她很熱情（她很騷）

〔註2〕：指辛辣的

例：The pepper is hot.

辣椒很辣。

〔註3〕：【俗語】麻煩

Give it him hot!

對他予以嚴責。

〔註4〕：指熱的。

例：A hot day

熱天

※10. had better

〔註〕：【非正式】用語。最好，應該，必須。

should；must。

例1. I had better leave now,or I'll be late.

我最好現在離開，否則會遲到。

2. If you want to stay out of trouble,you had better not make any mkstakes.

如果你不想惹麻煩，最好不要有任何錯誤。

※11. hand in（或turn in）

〔註〕：繳出，繳交作業。

例1. Professor asked the students to hand in their assignments.

教授要求學生交出作業。

2. Hand your papers in to me inside of three days.

三天內把你的學期報告交給我。

3. I want you to turn in a good history paper.

我要你繳出一篇好的歷史學期報告。

※12. hand in hand

〔註1〕：副詞片語。手牽著手，心連著心，1988年漢城奧運主題曲即"hand in hand"。

例：Bob and Mary walked along hand in hand in the park.

Bob和Mary手牽著手在公園散步。

〔註2〕：常與go連用，相伴隨，一起。

例：Selfishness和Unhappiness often go hand in hand.

自私和不快樂常是相伴隨的。

13. hand out

〔註〕：handout是指講義。hand out是分發東西之意。

例1. The teacher handed out the examination paper.
老師分發試卷給學生。

2. At the Christmas party Santa Claus handed out the presents under the tree.
聖誕節舞會，聖誕老公公在樹下分發禮物。

※14. hands off

〔註〕：【非正式】用語，放開手；不要碰我；不要煩我。
對付色狼的最佳用語。常用於命令語氣。

例1. Keep your hands off.
把你的手拿開。

2. Hands off me！
不要碰我！

3. I was going to touch the machine, but the man cried,“Hands off！”and I let it alone.
我正要碰觸機械，有人大叫“不要碰”，我連忙縮手。

※15. Hands up

〔註〕：【非正式】用語，把舉起手來。常見電視，電影片中，歹徒搶銀行或搶劫時命令語。

※16. Hang around

〔註〕：【非正式】用語，指逗留；消磨時間；鬼混。

例1. The principal warned the students not to hang around the corner drugstore after school.

校長警告學生下課後不要在藥局附近逗留。

2. Jim hangs around with some boys who live in his neighborhood.

Jim和住在附近鄰居的一些男孩鬼混。

※17. hang on

〔註〕：常用口語。抓緊或支持，撐住。

例1. Hang on！

抓緊（別鬆手）

2. Jack almost fell off the cliff,but managed to hang on until help came.

Jack幾乎掉下懸崖，但他設法抓緊直到救兵到。

18. hardly ever（或scarcely ever）

〔註〕：幾乎沒有，非常少，很少。

例1. It hardly ever snows in.Florida.

佛羅里達州幾乎不下雪。

2. John hardly ever reads a book.

John幾乎未曾看過一本書。

※19. hard-nosed

〔註〕：adj.【俚語】即Tough；難纏的；嚴格的；頑固的；特別是指在打鬥或比賽時。

例：Peter is a good boy;he plays hard-nosed football.

Peter是好男孩；他玩激烈的美式足球。

20. School of hard knocks

〔註〕：名詞片語，指學校或大學以外的生活經驗，即所謂的社會經驗。

例：He never went to high school;he was educated in the school of hard knocks.
他未上過高中，他受過社會經驗的磨練。

21. have been around

〔註〕：動詞片語。【非正式】用語，指經驗豐富的過來人。到過許多地方，認識許多人，做過許多事，見識廣博的人。

例1. It's not easy to fool him;he's been around.
他是見識廣博的人，不容易騙他。

2. Bob likes to go out with Jerry,because he has been around.
Bob喜歡跟Jerry出去，因為他見識廣博。

※22. have to（或have got to）

〔註〕：【非正式】用語。must；need to。必須，指有義務。

例1. Do you have to go now？
你必須現在走嗎？

2. I have got to go to the doctor.
我必須去看醫師。

3. I have to go to Church.
我必須到教堂去。

23. have to do with

〔註〕：動詞片語，指與有關係。

例：The book has to do with airplanes.
這本書的內容與飛機有關。

24. head-hunting

〔註〕：【俚語】，【俗語】獵尋人才，如星探，到

處發掘明星。head-hunting是大企業公司派人找尋適當人才。

例：The president sent a committee to the colleges and universities to do some head hunting; we hope he finds some young talent.
董事長指派特別小組到各大專院校找尋人才，我們希望他能發現一些年青高材生。

※25. head out

〔註〕：【非正式】用語，指離開或即將出發。

例1. I got to head out.
我該走了。

2. Hey, you guys, where're you head out to?
喂各位，你們去那裡？

3. I have a long way to go before dark.
I'm going to head out.
天黑前我要趕很長的路，現在我要走了。

4. The ship left port and headed out to sea.
船離開碼頭，駛向海洋。

26. head up

〔註〕：【非正式】用語，成為領導者或成為老闆。

例：Mr. Jones will head up the new business.
Jones先生將掌管新的事業。

27. heart-to-heart

〔註〕：形容詞。心連心，即坦誠的。

例：The father decided to have a heart-to-heart talk with his son about smoking.
父親決定坦誠的與他兒子討論抽菸的事。

※28. hit-and-run

〔註〕：指駕車撞到人後即逃之夭夭之人。

例：a hit-and-run driver
肇事後即行逃逸的司機。

29. hit the books

〔註〕：動詞片語。【非正式】用語，準備功課，學習功課。

例：I've got to hit the books.
我必須要準備功課了。

※30. hit the sack

〔註〕：動詞片語，【俚語】。指上床睡覺。

例1. I want to hit the sack.
我要去睡覺了。

2. Louis was so tired that he hit the sack soon after supper.
Louis太累以致晚飯後就睡覺了。

3. The man hit the sack early,in order to be out hunting at down.
為了黎明時出外打獵，這個人提早睡覺休息。

※31. hit the road

〔註〕：動詞片語。【俚語】，指離開，特別是指車子，動身出發，起身。

例1. It is getting late,so I guess we will hit the road for home.
天色漸暗，我想我們該動身回家了。

2. He packed his car and hit the road for California.
他把車裝載好後動身出發到加州。

32. hit the sauce

〔註〕:動詞片語。【俚語】大量或成癮的喝酒類飲料。

例:When Sue left him,Joe begin to hit the sauce.

Joe開始嗜酒,當Sue離開他以後。

33. hit the spot

〔註〕:動詞片語,【非正式】用語,指提神,特別是食物或飲料。

例:A cup of tea always hits the spot when you are tired.

當你疲倦時,一杯茶常可提神。

34. hog-tie

〔註〕:動詞。【非正式】用語,指把動物綁緊,使不能動或逃走。

例:The cowboy caught a calf and hog-tied it.

牛仔捉住一頭小牛並把它綁緊。

※35. hold good

〔註〕:有效期限

例1. The coupon held good only till the end of the year.優待券只到年底前有效。

2. The agreement between the schools held good for three year.

學校間的合約三年有效。

※36. hold it

〔註〕:動詞片語。【非正式】用語。"站住別動",
"等一下",常用於命令。阻止某人做某

事。警匪槍戰影片中，警察對著正逃跑的歹徒吆喝道〝Hold it〞站住，否則你命休矣。

例：The pilot was starting to take off when the control tower ordered "Hold it!"

當控制台命令〝等一下〞時，駕駛員正準備起飛。

※37. hold on

〔註1〕：【非正式】用語。電話中常用，請稍後，稍等。接電話時請對方稍後，即wait a minute；just a minute同。

例：Mr. Jones asked me to hold on while he spoke to his secretary.

Jone先生要我稍等一下，當他對他秘書說話時。

〔註2〕：常用於命令，等一下之意。

例："Hold on!" Bob's father said, "I want the car tonight."

Bob的父親說，"等一下"，"今晚我要用車。"

38. hold one's breath

〔註〕：動詞片語。當緊張或興奮時，屏息靜候，暫停呼吸。

例：The race was so close that everyone was holding his breath at the finish.

賽跑比賽太接近，以致快到終點時每個人都屏息靜候。

※39. hold up

〔註1〕：【非正式】用語。搶劫，電視，電影片中常見歹徒持槍搶劫銀行時用語。It's hold up！這是搶劫，快把錢拿出，否則沒命。

例：Masked man held up the bank.

蒙面人搶劫銀行。

〔註2〕：舉起，舉高

例：John held up his hand.

John舉起他的手。

〔註3〕：支持，攜帶。

例：The chair was too weak to hold up Mrs. Smith.

椅子太脆弱以致不能撐住Smith太太的體重。

40. home run

〔註〕：全壘打。棒球比賽時擊出的全壘打。

例：Frank hit a home run over the left field wall in the second inning.

Frank在第二局比賽時，擊出了左外野牆的全壘打。

41. honey moon is over

〔註〕：蜜月期結束。指兩個人或兩組組織首次的友誼或合作親密關係結束，可能已失去互相利用的價值。

例1. The honeymoon was soon over for the new foreman and the men under him.

新領班和他手下親密關係很快就結束了。

2. A few months after a new President is elected, the honeymoon is over and Congress and the President begin to criticize each other.

新總統選舉完幾個月後，總統和國會的親密關係就結束了，並開始互相抨擊。

※42. how about（或what about）

〔註〕：介系詞。怎麼樣？如何？常用於詢問決定，意見，解釋，作為等。

例1. How about another piece of pie？
再來一片餡餅，怎麼樣？

2. Will you lend or give me？
How about five dollars until Friday？
借給我或者給我呢？借五塊錢星期五還怎麼樣？

3. How about going to the dance with me Saturday？
星期六和我去跳舞怎麼樣？

※43. how come

〔註〕：【非正式】用語。口語中常用。同why，為什麼，怎樣發生的。即How does（did）it come that之簡稱。

例1. How come you are late？
你為什麼遲到了呢？

2. Yor're wearing your best clothes today. How come？
你今天穿這麼漂亮的衣服，為什麼？（是否有特別原因，約會，相親。）

II. 常用短句，格言，句型練習

44. Q:How do you want your coffee？

A:Cream and sugar,please.
問:你要怎樣的咖啡？

答:請加糖和奶精。

〔註〕:歐美人士喝咖啡非常普遍，個人喜好不同，有的咖啡不加糖，奶精，即Black coffee.有的只加sugar，有的則只加cream。

45. How long have you been studying in the United States?

你在美國求學有多久?

〔註〕:What are you planning to study in the United States?

你打算在美國讀什麼?

等諸如此類的話題，留學生最常被問到的問題，不管是朋友，同學甚至是移民局官員。初抵美國對自己留學的動機是什麼應最好心裡有數，不要只為留學而留學。

※46. Have a nice day!(或Have a good day)

〔註〕:每天見面或分別時，禮貌的問候語。每天常用口語。可以簡單回答，same to you.或you too即你也一樣。

47. Have a fun.(=Have a good time)

〔註〕:好玩的，快樂時光，玩得很愉快。

※48. Have a nice trip!

〔註〕:祝旅途愉快!對即將遠行的人祝福語。

49. Hello,there.

〔註〕:嗨。打招呼用語。

50. Here we go!

我們開始吧!

〔註〕:催促提醒別人即將開始。

2-5　PART（Ⅰ）

Ⅰ・常用單字，俚語，俗語

※1. Impressed

〔註〕：有印象的，效果的。對某人某事的觀感。
impress為常用動詞。

例1. I was impressed with Frank's personal charm,good sense of humor.
我對Frank吸引的外表和幽默感留下深刻印象。

2. His speech made a strong impression on the audience.
他的演說給觀衆留下深刻印象。

2. If only

〔註〕：即I wish，我希望之意

例1. If only it would stop raining.
我希望停止下雨。

2. If only Mother could be here.
我希望母親能在這裡。

3. in addition

〔註〕：副詞片語。除……之外。

例1. In addition to my studies,I got involved in lots of extracurricular activities.
除了讀書外，我還參加許多課外活動。

2. He has two cars and in addition a motoboat.
他有兩輛車子，除外還有一艘汽船。

※4. in advance

〔註〕：預先，預約。像預訂機票，旅館，車票等。

例：The motel man told Mr. williams he would have to pay in advance.

汽車旅館的人告訴William先生須預付房間費。

5. in and out

〔註〕：副詞片語。進進出出。

例：He was very busy saturday and was in and out all day.

星期六他非常忙碌，整天進進出出。

6. in any case

〔註〕：副詞片語。不管任何情況下，不論如何。

例1. It may rain tomorrow,but we are going home in any case.

明天可能會下雨，但不管如何我們還是回家去。

2. I may not go to Europe,but in any case,I will visit you during the summer.

我可能不會到歐洲去，但不論如何，我暑假一定去拜訪你。

7. in behalf of（或on behalf of）

〔註〕：當介詞。代表，為正式用法。

例：John accepted the championship award in behalf of the team.

John代表團隊接受冠軍獎。

※8. In brief（同In short;In a word）

〔註〕：副詞片語。簡而言之，簡要的，摘要。指給予口頭或書面上的摘要。

例：The speaker didn't know his subject, nor did he speak well;In brief,he was disappointing.
演說者不知道他的主題，亦說得不好，簡單的說，他太令人失望了。

9. In case

〔註1〕介系詞。有if之意，假如；如果。

例1. I stayed home in case you called.
如果你打電話，我會在家裡。

2. What shall we do in case it snows？
如果下雪我們該怎麼辦？

※10. in charge

〔註1〕：形容詞片語。掌管；控制；負責。

例：If you have any questions,ask the boss. He's in charge.
如果你有任何問題，問老板，他負責一切。

※〔註2〕：in charge of當介詞用。負責，掌管…事

例1. Marian is in charge of selling tickets.
Marian負責售票工作。

2. Who is in charge of this office？
這辦公室誰負責？

3. The girl in charge of refreshments forget to order the ice cream for the party.
負責點心部份的女孩，忘了訂購冰淇淋供舞會使用。

※11. in common

〔註1〕：副詞片語。相同；相似

例1. We have something in common.
我們某方面有些相似的地方。

2. The four boys grew up together and have a lot in common.
這四位男孩在一起長大而有許多相似點。

〔註2〕：共同擁有

例：Mr. and Mrs. Smith own the store in common.
Smith先生和太太共同擁有這家商店。

※12. in fact

〔註〕：副詞片語。常用口語，即事實上，通常用於強調事實。

例：It was a very hot day;in fact,it was 100° F degrees.
這是個大熱天，事實上有華氏100° 之高。

※13. in favor of

〔註〕：喜愛，有利的，讚同，讚成。

例1. Everyone in the class voted in favor of the party.
班上每一位同學投票贊成舞會。

2. Most girls are in favor of wearing lipstick.
大多數女孩子喜歡帶唇膏。

14. in front of

〔註〕：當介詞。在…前面，前面。

例1. A big Oak tree stood in front of the building.
大橡樹聳立在建築物前面。

2. The rabbit was running in front of the dog.
兔子跑在狗的前面。

15. in general

〔註〕：副詞片語。通常，一般說來；大體上，同 generally；generally speaking

例1. In general, mother makes good cookies.
通常，母親會做好吃的小餅干。

2. Generally,a garden is more beaufiul than a parking lot.
通常來說，花園是比停車場美麗。

3. Generally speaking, shoes are more expensive than socks.
通常說來，鞋子比襪子貴。

16. in honor of

〔註〕：敬意；紀念；敬愛

例1. We celebrate Mother's day in honor of our mothers.
我們慶祝母親節，對母親表示敬意。

2. The city dedicated a monument in honor of the general.
本市奉獻紀念碑，來紀念將軍。

※17. in line

〔註〕：副詞片語。排隊，排成一條線。歐美人士從小就養成排隊的習慣，不論是等車，買票，上餐廳，守法習慣值得國人借鏡。

※例1. Excuse me, are you in line?
對不起，你在排隊嗎？

2. A lot of people are standing in line, they are waiting to buy their. lunch.
許多人排隊，他們正等著買午餐。

3. The boys stood in line to buy their ticket.
男孩子們排隊買票。

18. in memory of

〔註〕：紀念某人或某事

例1. The building was named Ford Hall in memory of a man named James Ford.
名為Ford Hall的建築物是為紀念名叫James Ford的人。

2. Many special ceremonies are in memory of famous men.
許多特別紀念典禮是為了紀念名人。

※19. in order

〔註1〕：副詞片語。按…順序

例1. Line up and walk to the door in order.
排隊按順序走到門邊去。

2. Come to my desk in alphabetical order as I call your names.
當我叫名字時，按字母順序走到我桌子來。

〔註2〕：in order to為了，為了某種目的。

例1. We picked apples in order to make a pie.
我們摘蘋果為了做蘋果派。

2. In order to follow the buffalo,the Indians often had to move their camps.
為了跟蹤大水牛，印地安人常必須時常遷移。

20. in public

〔註〕：副詞片語，公開場合。

例：Actors are used to appearing in public.
演員慣常出現在大庭廣衆。

21. inside out

〔註〕：翻轉，內面跑到外面，如穿襪子，衣服穿反了。upsidedown是指上下顚倒。

例：Mother turns the stockings inside out when she washes them.
當母親洗襪子時把它翻轉過來。

※22. instead of

〔註〕：取代，做…而不。為托福聽力測驗常考句。

例1. The boys went fishing instead of going to school.
男孩子們去釣魚而不到學校去。

2. I wore mittens instead of gloves.
我戴四指連一起的手套而不是普通手套。

※23. in term of

〔註〕：當介詞。同about；especially about； In the matter of.
關於。常用於口語。

例1. He spoke about books in terms of their publication.
他談到書和特別有關出版的事。

2. What have you done in terms of fixing the house?
關於修房子你做了什麼？

3. The children ate a great many hot dogs at the party.In terms of money,they ate $20 worth.

宴會上小孩們吃了許多熱狗。關於錢的話，他們吃了約20美元。

24. in the clouds

〔註〕：形容詞片語。做夢；夢想；沉醉於。Far from real life；in dream。常與head,mind,thoughts連用。

例1. When Alice agreed to marry Jim,Jim went home in the clouds.

Jim回到家沉醉於美好未來，當Alice答應要嫁給他時。

2. Mary is looking out the window, not at the chalkboard; her head is in the clouds again.

Mary望著窗外，沒有注意黑板，他又心不在焉。

※25. in the long run

〔註〕：副詞片語。In the end最後，最後結果

例：John knew that he could make a success of the littel weekly paper in the long run.

John知道他最後能成功的辦好小型週報。

26. in time

〔註〕：形容詞片語，及時的

例1. We got to the station just in time to catch the bus.

我們及時趕到車站，正好趕上公車。

2. We go to Washington in time for the cherry

blossons.

我們到華盛頓正好趕上櫻花盛開。

27. in turn

〔註〕：副詞片語。論流，依照順序。

例1. Each man in turn got up and spoke.

每個人輪流起來講話。

2. Two teachers supervised the lunch hour in turn.

兩位老師輪流監督午餐。

II. 常用短句，格言，句型練習

※28. I mean.

〔註〕：我的意思是，我的想法是。為常用口語。

例 ：I mean,I don't know anything about medicine,right.

我的意思是我不懂醫學，好嗎？

29. I can't follow you.

我不明白你的意思。

〔註〕：對別人嘰嘰呱呱說個不停，聽不懂請其再說一次。

※30. I have no idea

〔註〕：我不知道，我不明白。同I don't know，口語常用。

※31. I don't care.

〔註〕：我不在乎。表示對事情的發展毫不關心。

Who cares？誰在乎？

I don't care？我才不在乎呢！

※32. I'll say

〔註〕:【非正式】用語。意指“我完全同意”,“我認為”,不可只照字面解釋。為常用口語。

例1. I'll say this is a good movie!
我認為這確實是一部好的電影。

2. Q:Did the children all enjoy Aunt Sally's apple pie?
A:I'll say!
問:孩子們都喜歡Sally舅媽的蘋果派嗎?
答:我想是的!

※33. I'm telling you.

〔註〕:【非正式】用語。我慎重告訴你,警告你,值得注意的。你聽我說,說話者加強說話的重要性。為常用口語,電視,電影集常可聽到的對話。

例1. Marian is a smart girl but I'm telling you, she doesn't always do what she promises.
Marian是聰明的女孩,但你聽我說,她並不是常守信用的。

※34. I'll tell you what(或Tell you what)

〔註〕:【非正式】用語。意指我有好主意,我有個構想。爲常用口語,必記。

例:The hamburger stand is closed, but I'll tell you what, Let's go to my house and cook some hot dogs.
漢堡店關門了,我有好主意,到我家去烤熱狗吃吧!

※35. I said A,as in apple.

我說A是蘋果Apple這字首的A。

〔註〕：如果有人不了解你說的英文單字字母時，可以念一個字母作參考。

例1. Q:What letter did you say ?I didn't understand you.

A:I said B,as in Banana.

問:你說的是那一個字母？我並不了解。

答:我說B，是香蕉Banana的B。

2. I said M,as in Mother.

我說M，是母親Mother的M。

※36. I have no choice.

我別無選擇。

〔註〕：如被歹徒用槍抵住時，別無選擇，只好任其行事，以保住小命。

37. I have finacial problem.

我手頭很緊。

〔註〕：指經濟有困難，學費快繳不出來。有錢走遍天下，無錢是寸步難行。

38. I want to call my lawyer.

我要找我的律師來。

〔註〕：美國是個民主國家，當警察逮捕嫌犯後必須告知嫌犯關於他的權利。除非有律師在場，嫌犯可以不回答任何問題。

You have the right to remain silent.

你有不發言的權利。（你有保持緘默的權利。）

39. I will do as you say.

我照著你的話做。

〔註〕：歹徒拿著槍對著你，命令把錢統統拿出來，只好照做否則小命休矣。

40. It's neat.

太好，太棒了。（很乾淨，清潔）

〔註〕neat【俚語】，Fine；wonderful，很棒之意。

※41. It's a deal.

一言為定。

〔註〕：與人商對事情，互作承諾。

※42. It's ridiculous.

這太莫明奇妙了。

〔註〕：指太荒謬了，太可笑的。

43. It's a long story.

說來話長，一言難盡。

44. It's a long way to go.

還有很長的路要走。

〔註〕：引申為仍須多加努力，革命尚未成功同志仍須努力。

45. I'll be there.

我將會準時到達。

〔註〕：答應某人到時將會赴約。

46. It's good to be home.

回到家真好。

〔註〕：所謂在家千日好，出門是事事難。

※47. It's not my day.

今天真倒霉，夠衰了。

〔註〕：辦事遇到阻礙或不順利時，抱怨語。
例如早上無原無故的挨老板一頓臭罵，It's not my day 夠衰了。

※48. It's up to you.

由你決定吧。

〔註〕：女友詢問今晚上館子吃飯如何？可答以上句，以討歡心。

49. Is that so?

真那樣嗎？

〔註〕：表同意的回答，等於Oh,indeed？或Oh, really？

50. Is there any pay phone around here?

這附近有公用電話嗎？

〔註〕：pay phone是指放入銅板使用的公用電話。

PART（J）

I・常用單字，俚語，俗語

1. Jaywalker

［dʒe͵wɔrkə］

〔註〕：【俗語】不遵守交通規則隨便穿越馬路的人，台北街頭到處可見。

2. Jailbait

〔註〕：【俚語】，指未成年的女子。所謂「幼齒」，在美國若與未成年的女子發生性關係要被判刑的。台灣目前也已有類似立法保障未成年兒童。

例：Stay away from Mary,she is a jailbait.
離開Mary遠一點，她尙未成年。

3. jeans

〔註〕：牛仔褲。時下年青人喜好的輕便裝。

※4. Jet log（n.）

〔註〕：由於時差及長途飛機旅行所引起的心理及生理不適應。如由台北飛芝加哥，時差約12小時抵達目的地即有日夜顚倒之感。

例：The jet log didn't show.
時差所引起的不適並未出現。

5. jerk

〔註〕：【俚語】愚笨，討厭的人。

例：He is jerk.

他是個討厭鬼。

※6. jogging

〔註〕：慢跑步。

例：As I was jogging,a man stopped me and asked for the time.

當我慢跑步時，有人攔住我問時間。

※7. junk food

〔註〕：所謂的垃圾食物，指一些較少營養價值的零食或低卡路里calories的食物。汽水，可樂，小餅干，零食之類。

※8. John Hancock

〔註〕：【非正式】用語。指簽名，your signature。原為人名為簽署獨立宣言者之一。Boston有一棟著名摩天大樓John Hancock Tower為華裔美人貝律銘建築師所設計。

例1. Put your John Hancock on this paper.

請你在這文件上簽名。

2. Joe felt proud when he put his John Hancock on his very first driver's license.

當Joe在首次拿到的駕駛執照上簽字時，感到很驕傲。

9. Jack up

〔註1〕以起重機抬起

例：The man jacked up his car to fix a flat tire.

這個人以起重機把車抬起修理漏氣的輪胎。

〔註2〕：【非正式】用語，哄抬物價。

例：Just before Christmas, some stores jack up their prices.
就在聖誕節前，有些商店哄抬物價。

10. join forces（或join hand）

〔註〕：指聯手合作，聯合。

例1. The student and graduates joined forces to raise money when the Gym burned down.
當體育館被燒毀時，學生和畢業生聯合募款。

2. American soldiers joined hands with the British in the war against Germany.
在對抗德國的戰爭中，美國士兵和英國士兵聯合作戰。

※11. jump to a conclusion

〔註〕：動詞片語，不假思索即遽下結論，常用口語。

例：Jerry saw his dog limping on a bloody leg and jumped to the conclusion that it had been shot.
Jerry看到他的狗，腳流血跛行，即遽下結論說牠被射傷的。

12. just about

〔註〕【非正式】用語。almost；幾乎；近乎。

例1. Just about everyone in town came to hear the mayor speak.
幾乎鎮上的每一個人都去聽市長演說。

2. Q:Has Mary finished peeling the potatoes?
A:Just about.
問:Mary已經剝完馬鈴薯的皮嗎？
答:快了。

PART（K）

Ⅰ．常用單字，俚語，俗語

※1．kid

〔註〕：【非正式】用語。A child，指小孩子，常用於口語。

例：I'm not a kid, I'm a man.
我不是小孩，我是大人了。

2．know-it-all

〔註〕：萬事通，什麽都知道的人。

例1．After George was elected as class president, he wouldn't take suggestions from anyone; he become a know-it-all.
George當選為班代表後，他不接受任何人的建議；他成了萬事通。

2．The others students didn't like George's know-it-all attitude.
其他同學不喜歡George萬事通的態度。

3．kickback

〔註〕：【俚語】，回扣，賄賂等。不肖官商勾結私相收受金錢禮物等。

例：He was arrested for making kickback payments.
他因賄賂被捕了。

※4．keep an eye on（或keep one's eye on）

〔註〕：動詞片語，小心看顧，看管著，特別注意。口語常用

例1. Park it here,I'll keep an eye on it.
把車停這裡，我會好好看管它。

2. A good driver keeps his eye on the road.
優良駕駛特別小心注意道路。

3. Keep an eye on the stove in case the coffee boils.
注意爐火以免咖啡煮沸了。

4. Just keep an eye on the road.
注意路面，小心駕駛。

5. keep company

〔註〕：動詞片語，作伴。

例：I'll go shopping with you just to keep you company.
我跟你一起逛街只是跟你作伴。

※6. keep in mind

〔註〕：記住，特別注意，記在心裡不要忘了。

例1. Keep in mind the rules of safety when you swim.
當你游泳時記住安全規則。

2. You have to be home by 11 o'clock. Keep that in mind.
你必須11點以前回到家，記住不要忘了。

※7. keep on（或go on）

〔註〕：繼續做某事，不要停頓。

例1. He keeps on talking all the time.

他一直講個不停。

2. Columbus kelp on until he saw land.
哥倫布繼續前進直到發現陸地。

※8. keep one's mouth shut

〔註〕：【非正式】用語。同shut up；閉嘴；保持肅靜。常用於命令，較不客氣的表示法。對別人喋喋不休表示不滿可用之。

例：Keep your mouth shut !
你給我閉嘴！

9. kick down

〔註〕：動詞片語。【俚語】把汽車，吉甫車或貨車從高擋轉入低擋。

例：Joe kicked the jeep down from third to second;and we slowed down.
Joe把吉甫車從三擋轉入二擋，我們才慢下來。

10. kick it

〔註〕：動詞片語。【俚語】，踢除，排除惡習慣，如喝酒，抽菸，毒癮等。

例：Bob finally kicked it;he's in good shape.
Bob終於排除惡習，他現在有好的身材。

11. kick off

〔註1〕：【非正式】用語。即To begin；Launch；start，開始之意。

例：The candidate kicked off his campaign with a speech on television.
候選人利用電視演說，開始他的競選活動。

〔註2〕：開球。足球賽踢球開始比賽。

例：John kicked off and the football game started.
John踢球開始足球比賽。

※12. kick out

〔註〕：把別人趕走或革職。常用於口語。

例：The boys made so much noise at the movie that the manager kicked them out.
男孩子在電影院吵得太厲害，經理把他們趕出戲院。

※13. kick the bucket

〔註〕：動詞片語。【俚語】，即To die，死了，照字面上看是踢到水桶，事實上是指pass away，死去之意。美國人較含蓄，有些字眼喜用別的字取代。

例：Old Mr. John kicked the bucket just two days before his ninety-fourth birthday.
John老先生94歲生日前兩天死了。

※14. kind of（或sort of）

〔註〕：副詞片語。【非正式】用語。常用於口語。幾乎是；不全然，即rather ;a little.

例1. Bod was kind of tired when he finished the job.
做完工作後，Bob有一些疲倦。

2. A guinea pig looks kind of like a rabbit，but it has short ears.
天竺鼠看起來像兔子，但牠的耳朵短。

3. The teacher sort of frowned but then smiled.
老師皺了一下眉頭，然後笑了。

15. Knock oneself out

〔註〕：動詞片語。【非正式】用語。努力工作；認真工作；盡力。

例：Tom knocked himself out to give his guests a good time.

Tom盡力使客人有愉快的時光。

※16. Knock out

〔註〕：動詞片語。拳賽擊倒對方，使動彈不得。常用口語。

例1. The champion knocked out the challenger in the third round.

衛冕者在第三回合把挑戰者擊倒。

2. Joe knocked hin out with one punck.

Joe一拳將他擊倒。

II. 常用短句，格言，諺語

※17. Knock it off！（或Cut it out）

〔註〕：【俚語】，阻止別人揶揄或說風涼話。制止，停止，之意。常用口語，必記。

例：Come on Joe knock it off, you're not making any sense at all.

算了吧，Joe，別講了，你從來不講正經話的。

18. Kill two birds with one stone.

〔註〕：【格言】，與中文一箭雙鵰，或一石二鳥同義。

例：Mother stopped at the supermarket to buy bread and then went to get Jane at dancing

class；she killed two birds with one stone.
母親到超級市場買麵包，順道到舞蹈教室帶Jane回家，她真是一箭雙鵰。

PART（L）

Ⅰ.常用單字，俚語，俗語，非正式用語

1. Lady killer

〔註〕：【俗語】，指小白臉。討好女性的男人，諸如午夜牛郎。

例：Joe is a regular lady killer.
Joe是標準的小白臉。

2. lobbyist

〔註〕：遊說家。美國華盛頓國會山莊有許多公司專家，負責與政府機構打交道，這些遊說家的任務是盡力維護顧客利益，工作內容包括了解不利的法律條文，結合民衆整體利益。

※3. Leases

〔註〕：租約，合約，即contract。

例：When renting an apartemnt you usually have to sign a contract or lease.
當你租一間公寓時，通常你須簽一份租約。

4. Live show

現場表演，真人表演

〔註〕：電視上live是指現場播出，file指檔案照片。

※5. Lousy !

〔 'lauzɪ 〕

〔註〕：指差勁的人或事，不高明的。為常用口語。

例1. Lousy guy !

差勁的傢伙！

2. It's a lousy question.

這是很沒水準的問題。

6. Lottery

〔註〕：獎券，採券。嗜賭為人之本性，有人賭錢，有人賭命。大家樂，六和彩之盛行可見一般。

7. Last word

〔註〕：爭論最後的結果

例：I never win an argument with her,she always has the last word.

我總爭論不過她，她的話永遠說不完。

※8. Later on

〔註〕：當副詞，即Later，以後，將來之意。常用於口語。

例：Finish your lessons.

Later on,we may have a surprise.

完成你的學業，將來我們可能會感到驚奇的。

9. laugh off

〔註〕：一笑置之，不當一回事。not take seriously.

例1. You can't laugh off a ticket for speeding.

對超速罰單，你不能一笑置之。（你必須小心以免再受罰）

2. He had a bad fall while ice skating but he laughed it off.

溜冰時他摔了一大跤，但他不當一回事，一笑置之。

※10. Lay off

〔註1〕：解僱。公司不景氣時，老板最常用的手段，現在政府實施勞基法，隨便解僱員工，可能引起勞資糾紛。

例1. The company lost the contract for making the shoes and laid off half its workers.
公司失掉製造鞋子的合約，因而解僱一半的工人。

〔註2〕：【俚語】，停止騷擾，即Leave me alone.

例：Lay off me.will you？I have to study for a test.
別煩我，好嗎？我必須準備考試。

11. Lay on the line（或put on the line）

〔註1〕動詞片語，【非正式】用語，付給，提供付款。

例：The sponsors had to lay nearly a million dollars on the line to keep the show on TV.
贊助者必須提供將近一百萬元之款項維持電視節目。

〔註2〕：指告知實情，據實以告使無疑問。

例：I'm going to lay it on the line for you,paul. You must work harder if you want to pass.
Paul，我要老實告訴你，如果你想通過測驗，你必須要努力。

※12. let off steam（或blow off steam）

〔註1〕：使…放氣

例1. The Janitor let off some steam because the pressure was too high.
因為壓力太大了，工友把蒸氣放出。

〔註2〕：【非正式】用語，消除體力，強烈感覺，拿…出氣

例：After the long ride on the bus,the children let off steam with a race to the lake.
長途坐車後，小孩們跑到湖邊發洩體力。

※13. Let me see.

〔註1〕：讓我考慮一下或想一下【非正式】用語。會話時，一時無法回答時短暫的思考停頓，Let me see……或Well,……。

例：I can't come today.Let me see. How about Friday？
我今天不能來，讓我想一下，星期五怎麼樣？

〔註2〕：【非正式】用語，表現，讓我們知道

例：Let me see if you can jump over the fence.
表現給我看看是否你能跳過籬笆。

※14. lick one's boots

〔註〕：動詞片語。拍馬屁，討好，諂媚。所謂拍馬屁占上風。做任何事討好別人。

例：She wanted her boy friend to lick her boots all the time.
她要她的男朋友隨時討好她。

15. live from hand to mouth

〔註〕：動詞片語。指賺的少用的多，入不敷出，有捉襟見肘之意。

例：Mr. Johnson got very little pay,and the family lived from hand to mouth when he had no job.
Johnson先生收入很少，當他沒工作時，他的家庭就入不敷出。

16. live it up

〔註〕：【非正式】用語，尋樂。特別指比賽，夜生活等。

例：The western cowboys usually went to town on Saturdays to live it up.

西部牛仔通常在週末到鎮上尋樂。

※17. Lock up

〔註〕：動詞片語。【俚語】確定成功，保證成功。

例Q:How did your math test go？

A:I locked it up,I think.

問:你的數學測驗考的如何？

答:我想確定考得不錯。

18. look after

〔註〕：照顧，看顧，照料。

例1. John's mother told him to look after his younger brother.

John的母親告訴他要照顧他的小弟。

2. When he went to Europe,Mr. Jones left his son to look after the business.

當Jones先生到歐洲去時，他把兒子留下來照顧生意。

19. look back

〔註〕：回顧過去

例：As John looked back,his life seemed good to him.

當John回顧過去，他的一生對他似乎是美好的。

※20. look down on

〔註〕：動詞片語。輕視某人或某事，看不起別人。

例1. Jack looked down on AL for his poor manners.

Jack輕視AL不良的態度。

2. Miss Tracy likes tennis but she looks down on football as too rough.

Tracy小姐喜愛網球，但他輕視足球太粗魯。

※21. look forward to

〔註〕：期望，期待。

例：Frank was looking forward to that evening's. date.

Frank期待著晚上的約會。

※22. look up to

〔註〕：尊敬某人，敬佩。與look down on輕視，正好相反。常用片語。

例：Mr. Smith had taught for many years,and all the students looked up to him.

Smith先生已教書好幾年，所有的學生都尊敬他。

※23. look out（或watch out）

〔註〕：注意，小心之意。為常用口語，用於命令或警告。提醒別人小心，注意。

例1. "Look. out！" John called,as the car came toward me.

當車子駛向我時，John大叫，"小心"

2. Look out for the train！

小心火車！

24. look over

〔註〕：檢查，復習。

例1. I looked hurriedly over the apples in the basket and took one that looked good.
我很快的檢視籃子裡的蘋果，並挑選一個好的。

2. Mrs. Jones spent the evening looking over the months bills and writing checks.
Jones太太花了整晚時間查閱每月帳單再開支票。

25. Lose one's shirt

〔註〕：【俚語】指輸掉所有的錢，賠光了。

例1. Mr. Matthews lost his shirt betting on the horses.
Matthews先生賭馬輸掉了所有錢。

2. Uncle Joe spent his life savings to buy a store, but it failed,and he lost his shirt.
Joe叔叔花了他一生積蓄買了一家商店，但他失敗了，並且賠光所有的錢。

26. lose one's temper

〔註〕：發脾氣，大發雷霆。

例1. He lost his temper when he broke the key in the lock.
當他弄壞了上鎖的鑰匙時，大發脾氣。

※27. lose one's tongue

〔註〕：【非正式】用語。緊張或驚訝時，說不出話來，說話結結巴巴的。

例：The man would always lose his tongue when he was introduced to new people.
當他被介紹認識陌生人時，總是說不出話來。

28. lose sight of

〔註〕：動詞片語。失去蹤影，不再看見。

例1. I lost sight of Mary in the crowd.

在人群中我找不到Mary。

2. I watched the plane go higher and higher until I lost sight of it.

我望著飛機越飛越高直到看不見。

II. 常用短句，格言，句型練習

※29. Like what?

比方什麼

〔註〕：不明白別人所說的事物，請求舉例說明的發問語。

※30. Let's go!

我們走吧！

〔註〕：表示間接的命令。

※31. Leave me alone!

別管我！

〔註〕：心裡生氣時，不希望別人打擾。Please leave me alone！對別人的嘮叨表示不耐煩。

32. like father, like son

〔註〕：同中國成語，有其父必有其子。

例：Mr. Jones and Tommy are both quiet and shy.

Like father, like son.

Jone先生和Tommy兩人很文靜且愛羞，真是有其父必有其子。

※33. live and learn

〔註〕：【格言】活到老，學到老。所謂學無止境。

例1. "Live and learn" ,said mother.

"I never knew that the Indians once had a camp where our house is."

〝活到老，學到老〞，母親說：〝我未曾知道印地安人曾紮營在我們住的地方。〞

※34. What's your line?

請問你是從事那一行的？

〔註〕：這裡Line指occupation或trade之意。

例：It's not my line.

這不是我本行。

※35. Long time, no see.

〔註〕：好久不見。情人不見一日如隔三秋。

2-6 PART（M）

I・常用單字，俚語，俗語

1. Mid-term Exam

〔註〕：美大學的期中考試。Final Exam期末考。

※2. Marvelous！

棒極了，好極了！

〔註〕：為常用口語，稱讚別人外表或智慧。

例：You look marvelous！

你看起來真棒！

※3. make sense

〔註〕：合理的。make no sense不合理的。

例1. That doesn't make sense to me.

那對我不合理。

2. Does it make sense to let little children play with matches.

讓小孩玩火柴合理嗎？

4. Marihaana

[mærə'wanə]

〔註〕：大麻煙。所謂的毒品，全世界禁止吸食。其他常見毒品，cocain；dop;drug等。

5. Merry Christmas！

〔註〕：聖誕節快樂。聖誕節對歐美人士是一個重大節日。Christmas day每年12月25日，基督徒為紀念二千年前，耶穌基督誕生的節日，

現已風行全世界。

※6. **majority leader**

〔註〕：名詞。多數黨領袖，即國會有多數投票權的領袖。

例：The majority leader of the House of Representatives tried to get the members of his party to support the bill.
衆議院的多數黨領袖企圖說服他的同僚支持他的法案。

7. **make a difference**

〔註〕：有關係的，重要的

例1. It makes a difference how you do it.
你怎麼做是有關係的。

2. It doesn't make any difference to me.
這對我毫無關係。

8. **make a face**

〔註〕：動詞片語，【非正式】用語。做鬼臉，To twist your face.

例：The boy make a face at his teacher when She turned here back.
當老師轉過頭去時，男生向她做鬼臉。

9. **make away with**

〔註〕：【非正式】帶走，取走。Take；carry away

例：Two masked men held up the clerk and made away with the pay roll.
二個蒙面人搶劫職員並取走了薪資款項。

10. **make believe**

〔註〕：假裝。pretend

例1. Let's make believe we have a million dollars.
讓我們假裝我們有一百萬元。

2. Danny make believe he didn't hear his mother calling.
Danny假裝沒有聽到他媽媽在叫他。

11. make ends meet

〔註〕：片語。量入為出，即To have enough money to pay your bill.

例：Both husband and Wife had to work to make ends meet.
夫妻倆必須一同工作才能量入為出。

※12. make friends

〔註〕：交朋友。

例：You can make friends with an elephant by giving him peanuts.
你只要給大象花生，便可與牠做朋友。

13. make fun of

〔註〕：【非正式】用語。開玩笑，取笑，To joke about；tease。

例：Jame made fun of the new student because her speech was not like the other student.
Jame取笑新的同學因她說話不像其他的同學。

14. make good

〔註1〕：工作表現良好，成功，努力。

例：Bob make good as a salesman, and now he owns his own business.

Bob當推銷員工作努力，現在他已擁有自己的事業。

〔註2〕：實現諾言。

例：Smith borrowed some money. He promised to pay it back on pay day.
He made good his promise.
Smith借了一些錢，他答應領薪水時再還，他很守信用。

15. make it snappy

〔註〕：【非正式】用語，快一點；快走。常用於命令，To move quickly；hurry。

例：Make it snappy, or well be late for the movie.
快一點，否則我們會錯過電影。

※16. make oneself at home

〔註〕：常用客套語（主人待客時必用語）。用於請客人不要太拘束，像在自己家一樣。

例1. Make youself comfortable at home.
不必拘束，像在自己家一樣。

2. If you get to my house before I do, help yourself to a drink and make yourself at home.
如果你先抵達我家，不要客氣自己取用飲料。

※17. make a mistake

〔註〕：做錯事；犯錯誤；失誤。

例：You made a mistake about the time.
你記錯了時間。

2. You made a mistake in trusting him too much.

你錯在過份信任他。

18. make one's way

〔註〕：片語，為生活努力，開路，奮勇前進。

例：He was anxious to finish school and make his own way in the world.

他急著畢業開創自己的前途。

※19. make out

※〔註1〕：【非正式】用語。做成功，做的很好。為常用口語必記。

例1. How did you make out?

你是如何做成功的？

2. The sick woman could not make out alone in her house, so her friend came and helped her.

這女病患在家裡不能單獨做好任何事，所以她的朋友來幫她。

〔註2〕：試著努力去看，聽，了解清楚。

例1. It was dark, and we could not make out who was coming along the road.

太暗了，我們看不清楚誰延著大路走來。

2. The book had many hard words, and Anne could not make out what the writer meant.

這本書有許多艱深的字，Anne不了解作者的真意。

〔註3〕：指接吻或愛撫。

例：問：What are Jack and Jill up to？
Jack和Jill正在幹嗎？
答：They're making out on the back porch.
他們正在後陽台擁吻。

※20. make love

〔註〕：指作愛，有性行為的關係。

例：It is rumored that Dick makes love to every girl he hires as a secretary.
謠傳Dick與他僱用當秘書的每一位女孩作愛。

※21. make sure

〔註〕：動詞片語，確定，肯定，確信。

例：Father makes sure that all the lights are off before he goes to bed.
父親確定在他睡覺前把所有燈都關掉了。

※22. make up

〔註1〕：考試補考，補充。

例：I have to make up the test I missed last week.
我必須參加上星期缺席的補考。

〔註2〕：和好，吵架以後從修舊好。

例：Mary and Joan quarreled,but make up after a.while.
Mary和Joan吵架，但不久就從修舊好。

〔註3〕：化妝，塗脂粉。

例1. Tom watched his sister make up her face for her date.
Tom看著他妹妹化妝赴約會。

2. I don't like to see women make up in public.
我不喜歡看女人當衆化妝。

※23. make up one's mind

〔註〕：動詞片語，下定決心。為常用口語，決定。
即To choose what to do；decide。

※例1. I made up my mind.
或My mind is made up.
我已下定決心。（沒有人能改變我的心意）

2. They made up their minds to sell the house.
他們下定決心賣掉房子。

24. make way

〔註〕：動詞片語。讓路，避開，靠邊站。

例：The people make way for the king.
老百姓讓路給國王經過。

※25. matter of fact

〔註〕：名詞片語，即事實上，強調事實。

例1. I didn't go yesterday,and as a matter of fact,I didn't go.all week.
我昨天沒有去，事實上，我整個星期都沒去。

2. It is a matter of fact that the American war against England was successful.
事實上美國對抗英國的戰爭是成功的。

26. Miss out

〔註〕：【非正式】用語。To fail；not take a good chance.失敗，錯失良機。

例：You missied out by not coming with us;we had a great time.

你錯失艮機未與我們同行；我們玩得好愉快。

※27. Mix up

〔註〕：To confuse；make a mistake，迷惑，做錯了，誤認。

例1. Even the twins'mother mixes them up.
甚至是雙胞胎的母親也弄混了。

2. Jimmy doesn't know colors yet,he mixes up purple with blue.
Jimmy還不懂顏色，他誤認紫色為藍色。

28. more or less

〔註〕：副詞片語。多少有一些，大部份。即 somewhat；mostly。

例：Betty made some mistakes on the test,but her answers were more or less right.
Betty考試時有些答錯，但大部份答案是對的。

II. 常用短句，句型練習

※29. You make me sick!

你令我噁心

〔註〕：看不慣某人的作法，表示厭惡，半老徐娘仍裝作十八歲姑娘打扮，令人噁心。

30. May I help you!

我可以效勞嗎！（歡迎光臨之意）

〔註〕：服務人員，店員招呼顧客必用語。

※31. May I have your attention,please.

各位請注意！

〔註〕：機場，公衆場合，有重要事情廣播或提醒大

家注意。

32. I missed you very much.

我非常想念你。

〔註〕：miss動詞，當懷念，想念，思念。對女朋友或好友表示思念之意。

I missed you.

※33. me know

我知道

〔註〕：按照文法是不可以，但是老美有時在口語喜歡用me代I使用

例：Me do it.

我做成了。

PART（N）

Ⅰ. 常用單字，俚語，俗語

※1. No problem

沒問題，沒關係。

〔註〕：朋友請求幫忙，代為照顧女友，義不容辭，No problem包在我身上。

例：問：Can you handle that?

答：No problem,I can handle.

※2. No way

不行；不可以；休想。

〔註〕：常用口語。沒有辦法。遇到賴皮鬼要賴借錢，No way休想！

3. night life

〔註〕：名詞片語。夜生活，夜間的娛樂，觀光客最樂於消磨時間的娛樂。

例：People in the city are able to find more night life than those who live in the country.

住在城裡的人比住鄉下的人容易找到夜生活。

※4. no use

〔註〕：沒有用的；別白費力氣；徒勞無功。

例：Bob:Let's try again!

Dick:It's no use.

Bob:讓我們再試一下吧！

Dick:沒有用的啦。

5. No comments

〔註〕：無可奉告。政府官員答覆記者追問最常用語。comment是批評，談論之意。

例：You comments and directions are welcome.
歡迎批評指教。

6. no-show

〔註〕：當名詞。【俗語】指一些預訂旅社或航空公司機票，而後既沒有兌現又無取消的人。

例：The airlines were messed up because of a great number of no-show passemgers.
因為許多預定機票沒有兌現又無取消的旅客，把航空公司弄糊塗了。

※7. no good

〔註〕：不好，不適合。

例1. That's no good.
那樣做不好。

2. He was no good at arithmetic.
他算術方面不好。

※8. no doubt

〔註〕：副詞。毫無疑問地，確實地。

例：No doubt Susan was the smartest girl in her class.
毫無疑問地，Susan是班上最聰明的女孩。

※9. Not bad（或not so bad）

〔註〕：【非正式】用語。很好；不錯，還好過得去之意。即pretty good；all right；good enough。

例1. Q:How're you doing？

A:Not bad,an you？

問:近來好嗎？

答:還好，你呢？

2. The party last night was not bad.

昨晚的舞會還不錯。

10. No parking！

〔註〕：不准停車，小心被放氣。國人公德心是一流的差，佔用人行道，自家門前只要擺著No parking請勿停車，誰敢停車，車子準倒霉。

11. neither……nor（或neither……or）

〔註〕：常用連接詞，既不…亦不…

例1. We had niether money nor food.

我們既沒有錢亦沒有食物。

2. Neither John nor the twins know how to spell the word," alligator".

John和雙胞胎都不知如何去拼「alligator」這個字。

※12. never mind.

〔註〕：動詞片語。請勿介意，不要在意或對於別人的感激或道歉表示不在乎，算不了什麽，別放在心上。

同＝It doesn't mather.

＝Forget it.

＝Skip it.

＝Don't worry about it.

例：問：What did you say？

答：Oh, never mind.
問：你說什麼？
答：哦，算了沒什麼。

※13. never say die!

〔註〕：動詞片語，永不放棄，堅持到底。Don't quit：Don't be discourage永不灰心。

例："Never say die!" John said, as he got on his feet and tried to ice skate again.
John說，"不要灰心"，當他站起來再試著溜冰時。

14. next door

〔註〕：鄰居，隔壁。

例：He lived next door to me.
他住在我的隔壁。

15. no free lunch

〔註〕：沒有白吃的午餐，指天下無不勞而獲者。

16. no matter

〔註〕：不管如何，不論如何。

例1. He had to get the car fixed no matter how much it cost.
不管花多少錢，他必須把車子修好。

2. No matter what you try to do, it is important to be able to speak well.
不論你如何試著去做，最重要的是你要說得流利。

17. no sweat

〔註〕：【俚語】，容易完成的，不複雜的，容易的。easily。

例1. That job was no sweat.
那工作很容易做。
2. We did it,no sweat.
我們很容易地做成功了。（不費吹灰之力）

※18. Nothing further

〔註〕：沒有進一步的問題。「洛城法網」影集中，律師對證人的詰問毫不留情，直到滿意為止。Nothing further。

PART（O）

Ⅰ．常用單字，俚語，俗語，非正式用語

※1. obviously!

〔註〕：很明顯地，顯然地。常用口語，表示明顯的事實。

例：Obviously,he speak the truth.
明顯地，他說了真話。

2. open-minded

〔註〕：虛心的，能接受新觀念的，開放心胸。

※3. off-color

〔註〕：【非正式】，【俗語】，黃色笑話，尤指雙關語，開黃腔。off-color joke下流的笑話，對女同事少說off-color笑話，避免性騷擾嫌疑。

例：When Bob finished his off-color story, No one was pleased.
當Bob講完他的黃色故事，沒有人覺得高興。

※4. On-campus

〔註〕：校園；學校範圍內。off-campus則是校園以外。

5. On sale

〔註〕：廉售，大拍賣。百貨公司常用促銷產品的方法。

例：Tomato soup that is usually sold for twelve

cents a can is now on sale for ten cent.
蕃茄汁通常一罐賣12分錢現在大拍賣10分錢。

6. open up!

〔註〕：開門，把門打開。明知室內有人敲門仍不開時用語，發現歹徒躲在屋內，催促開門。

※6. of course

〔註〕：當然的，毫無疑問的。常用口語。

例1. Of course you know that girl;she is your classmate.
當然你認識那女孩，她是你同學。

2. 問：Do you work hard?
答：Of course I do.
問：你努力工作嗎？
答：當然我努力工作。

7. off and on

〔註〕：偶爾；occasionally；sometimes。

例：It rained off and on all day.
整天偶爾下著雨。

※8. on duty

〔註〕：上班；值班；執勤。off duty正好相反，指下班，不工作。

例1. Two soldiers are on duty guarding the gates.
二位阿兵哥正執勤守衛大門。

2. He goes on duty at 8 A.M. and comes off duty at 5 P.M.
他早上八點上班，下午五點下班。

9. off one's chest

〔註〕:【非正式】用語，一吐為快，把心中的話向別人傾訴。

例：After Bob told the teacher that he had cheated on the test, he was glad because it was off his chest.

當Bob把作弊的事告訴老師以後，他覺得很快樂，因他已一吐為快。

10. off the cuff

〔註〕:【非正式】用語，指即席演說，事前沒有特別的準備。

例：Some Presidents like to speak off the cuff to newspaper reporters, but others prefer to think questions over and write their answers.

有些總統喜歡面對新聞記者即席演說，但有些寧可仔細思考問題再寫下他們的答案。

※11. on account of

〔註〕:因為，結果。同Because of。

例1. He can not come to the meeting on account of illness.

他因病不能來開會。

2. The picnic was supposed to be held in the Gym on account of the rain.

因為下雨，野餐可能會在體育館舉行。

※12. Once in a while

〔註〕:Sometimes；occasionally；偶爾，有時候。

例：We go for a picnic in the park once in a

while.

我們偶爾到公園去野餐。

※13. Once upon a time

〔註〕：從前，很久很久以前，Long ago。常用於說故事的開頭語。

例：Once upon a time there lived a king who had an ugly daughter.

從前那裡住著一位國王，他有一位很醜的女兒。

14. On deposit

〔註〕：存款。存於銀行。

例：I have almost ＄300 on deposit in my account.

我有大約300美金存在我帳戶。

15. On foot

〔註〕：副詞片語，步行，走路，By walking。

例：Sally's car broke and she had to return home on foot.

Sally的車子壞了，她必須步行回家。

※16. on one's chest

〔註〕：形容詞片語。【非正式】用語，指使你困惑的心事，像女友不告而別。

例：You look sad. What's on your chest?

你看起來很傷心，到底有什麼心事？

※17. On purpose

〔註〕：副詞片語。故意地，not accidentally。

例1. The clown fell down on purpose.

小丑故意跌倒。

2. Jane did not forget her coat; she left it in

the locker on purpose.

Jane並沒忘掉她的外套；她故意把它放在衣櫃裡。

18. on schedule

〔註〕：副詞片語。按預定的計劃或時間，at the right time。

例1. The school bus arrived at school on schedule.

校車準時抵達學校。

2. The four seasons arrive on schedule each year.

每年四季按時來到。

※19. on the air

〔註〕：形容詞或副詞片語。指廣播電台或電視台，正廣播中。廣播節目中常聽到用語。

例1. His show is on the air at six o'clock.

他的表演在六點時播出。

2. The ballgame is on the air now.

球賽正在廣播中。

※20. on the button

〔註〕：【俚語】，指做的正是時候，正對時機，at the heart of matter

例：John's remark was right on the button.

John的評論正對時機。

※21. on the contrary

〔註〕：副詞片語。指正好相反，Exactly the opposite。

例1. 問：You don't like football,do you？
答：On the contrary,I like it very much.
問：你不喜歡美式足球，是嗎？
答：正好相反，我非常喜愛。
2. I thought that the children went to the zoo;on the contrary,they went to the park.
我想小孩子們會到動物園去；正好相反，他們去公園。

※22. on the other hand

〔註〕：副詞片語。另一方面，從另一個角度看。通常用於說明介紹相反或不同的事實或觀念。

例：Father and Mother wanted to go for a ride; the children,on the other hand,wanted to stay home and play with their friend.
父母親想要去兜風，但另一方面，孩子們卻想在家裡和朋友玩。

※23. on the rocks

〔註1〕：形容詞片語。【俚語】with ice only是加進冰塊而已。rock原是大石頭，rocks在此解作飲用的冰塊。指任何含酒精的飲料，on the rocks。

例1. Whisky on the rocks.
威士忌酒加冰塊。
2. At the restaurant,Sally ordered organge juice on the rocks.
Sally在飯店點了一份柳橙汁加冰塊。

〔註2〕：【非正式】用語，指船隻觸礁，或瀕臨毀滅

邊緣。

例：Mr Jone's business was on the rocks.

Jone先生的事業瀕臨破產。

24. on the side

〔註〕：副詞片語。【非正式】用語。指除了主要的事，數量外；即額外等。

例1. He ordered a hamburger with onions and French fries on the side.

他點了漢堡加洋蔥，另外加了炸薯條。

25. on the spot

〔註〕：【俚語】，死亡黑名單。謀殺的危險。

例：After he talked to the police, the gangstors put him on the spot.

他報警後，暴徒把他列入死亡黑名單。

※26. on the way（或on one's way）

〔註〕：形容詞或副詞片語。動身前往，出發往…途中，例如接到緊急電話，或命令即刻前往。常用於口語。即coming；going toward a place。

例1. I'll be on my way.

我馬上趕到。

2. Help was on the way.

救兵正在途中。

3. The train left and Bill was on his way to New York.

火車已離開，Bill正前往紐約的途中。

※27. on time

〔註〕：片語。準時。

例1. The train left on time.

火車準時開出。

2. Mary is alwasy on time for an appointment.

Mary一直都準時赴約。

※28. on top of the world

〔註〕：形容詞片語。【非正式】用語。同flying high快樂的感覺，覺得很有成就感。

例1. I was on top of the world when I found out that I got into college.

當我知道能進入大學就讀，我太興奮了。

※29. open fire

〔註〕：動詞片語。指開槍射擊，開火。

例1. When the cop called to the robber to stop, he turned and suddenly opened fire.

當警察喝令暴徒站住，暴徒突然轉身開槍射擊。

2. The big warship turned its guns toward the enemy ship and open fire.

大戰艦把砲口轉向敵艦並開火。

30. open one's heart

〔註〕：動詞片語。坦開心胸，坦誠的，坦白表明。

例1. John felt much better after he opened his heart to Betty.

John坦白面對Betty表明心跡後，他感覺舒服多了。

31. or so

〔註〕：大約，同about

例：The book cost $5 or so.

(＝It cost about $5.)

這本書約5塊美金。

※32. out of order

〔註〕：故障，壞掉不能使用。機械電器用品，像電視機，洗衣機，冰箱等，壞掉不能使用。

例1. Our television set is out of order.

我們的電視機壞了。

2. The elevator was out of order and we had to walk to the tenth floor.

電梯壞了，我們必須走到第十層樓去。

33. out of tune

〔註〕：尤指音樂變調，走音了。

例：The band sounded terrible, because the instruments were out of tune.

樂隊的聲音聽起來太糟了，因為樂器都變調了。

※34. over one's head

〔註〕：副詞或形容詞片語。難以理解的，無法了解，太難或奇怪的問題以致無法了解。

例1. The lesson today was hard; it went over my head.

今天的課太難了，我一點都不了解。

2. Mary laughed just to be polite, but the joke was really over her head.

Mary微笑只是為了禮貌，這個笑話她實在弄不明白。

PART（P）

I．常用單字，俚語，俗語

1. panties

女性的內褲

※2. A pain

指困擾，痛苦的經驗，爭論等。

〔註〕：【俚語】，pain，常用於口語，並非指真正的痛，感覺。

例1. Driving here is a pain.（塞車實在太厲害了）
同Driving here is difficult.（或struggle）
開車到這裡來真不容易。

2. That guy gives me a pain.
那傢伙跟我過不去。

3. parking lot

停車場。

4. page call

公衆場所以電話或廣播叫人的服務。

〔註〕：旅館，俱樂部，學校等以廣播喊出名字尋找（某人）。

例：Excuse me,can you page Room No 115 Mr. John for me,please.對不起，請幫我廣播找115房John先生。

5. pay day發薪日

〔註〕：上班族最樂的日子，pay check薪水支票。

※6. photographer

攝影師

〔註〕：photograph照片。

7. playboy

花花公子

〔註〕：【美俗】，指耽於遊樂，無所事事的富家子。美國著名雜誌”playboy”，則以拍裸體美女出名。

※8. positive

〔註〕：正面的，肯定的，好的結果。negative指負面的影響，結果。

※9. presentation

發表會，演講會。

10. practical training

〔註〕：留美獲得學位以後，可以申請一段時間工作許可以獲得實際經驗，大約是一年的時間。

※11. privacy

隱私權

〔註〕：美國人注重隱私權，最好避免詢問別人的年齡，婚姻或賺多少錢，以免自找沒趣。這是最不禮貌的。

例：He told me his reasons in strict privacy.
他極機密的告訴我他的理由。

12. pal

〔註〕：【非正式】用語，朋友，夥伴，同buddy。“Miami Vice”
警匪片影集中常可聽到的口頭語。

例：Hey！pal,what's up！
喂，老兄，還好吧！

13. picky

〔註〕：【非正式】用語，指愛挑剔的人，難以討好的人。hard to please。

例：He is picky.
他很挑剔。

14. pub

〔註〕：小酒館，小酒吧，同Bar

15. pull

〔註〕：拉出。門把上寫的字。提醒開門的人。push則是推，兩字常易混淆。

※16. pass.away

〔註〕：死去，die之意。

例：He passed away at eighty.
他在80歲時去逝。

※17. pass out

〔註〕：【非正式】，昏倒；失去知覺；faint。

例：She went back to work while she was still sick,and finally she just passed out.
她還生病就回去工作，最後終於昏倒了。

※18. pay for

〔註〕：因為做錯事，或沒有做而有麻煩。為…付出代價，罪有應得。為常用口語。例如某人好說謊，他日他將為說謊付出代價的。

例1. You'll pay for it.
你將得到報應。（付出代價）

2. When John could not get a good job, he realized he had to pay for all the years of fooling around instead of working in school.
John沒能找到好的工作，他才知道這是他在學校好玩沒有好好努力所要付出的代價。

19. pay one's way

〔註〕：以勞力賺取生活費

例：He paid his way by acting as a guide.
他當導遊賺取生活費。

※20. pick up

※〔註1〕：撿起來；拾起。

例：He picked up the stone and put it on the table.
他撿起石頭放在桌子上。

※〔註2〕：當接載；接送；搭載。

例1. I'll go to airport to pick you up.
我將到機場去接你。

2. I'll pick you up at 7 o'clock.
我七點來接你。

3. The bus stopped and picked up passengers.
公車停下來搭載旅客。

※〔註3〕：泡妞，指未經介紹而認識別人。尤指與異性交朋友，藉機搭訕，吊馬子。

例：Let's go to pub to pick up girl！
我們到酒廊去泡妞吧！

※〔註4〕：學習，學得。To learn

例：He never studied English, what he knows he

picked up while living in American.

他從未學過英文，他所會的英文是住在美國時學會的。

21. pitch in

〔註1〕：擲入，投入。常可見垃圾箱上寫的字，即將廢物投入，拋入。

〔註2〕：【非正式】用語，指努力工作。

例：Pitch in and we will finish the job as soon as possible.

努力工作我們將儘早完成工作。

22. play ball

〔 註 〕：指球類開始比賽，如桌球。

例：When umpire calls "play ball" ,the game begins.

當裁判叫"play ball" 比賽開始。

※23. play by ear

〔註1〕：【非正式】用語，即興的，隨機應變的，事先沒有計劃的。注意常與it一起連用。

例1. I play it by ear.

我臨時決定的。

2. John decided to play it by ear when he went for his interview.

當去面試時，John決定隨機應變。

24. play hooky

〔 註 〕：動詞片語。【非正式】，蹺課，逃學。

例：John is failing in school because he has played hooky so many times during the year.

John被當了，因為這學年他蹺課太多次了。

25. point out

〔註〕：用手指指出，清楚的指出位置。

例：The guide pointed out the main sights of the city.

導遊指出城市主要的參觀地點。

※26. polish the apple

拍馬屁，討好某人

〔註〕：動詞片語　【俚語】，apple polisher是馬屁精，好拍馬屁的人。

例1. Mary polished the apple at work because she wanted a day off.

Mary工作時拍馬屁，因為他想休假一天。

2. Bob is the teacher's pet because he always polishes the apple.

Bob是老師最寵的人，因他最會拍馬屁。

※27. port of entry

〔註〕：指入境關口。當你搭機抵達美國時是在芝加哥入境，移民局官員檢查護照，辦理入關手續。芝加哥即是你到美國的port of entry。

※28. pour out

〔註1〕：傾盆大雨，下很大的雨；To rain hard。

例：It's pouring out.

正下著傾盆大雨。

〔註2〕：指大量湧出的人潮

例：The people poured out of the building when they heard the fire alarm.

當人們聽到火警時，大量人潮湧出大廈。

※29. press conference

〔註〕：名詞片語。記者招待會。政府的施政，政策的轉達實有賴於大衆傳播媒體的轉達，溝通。

例1. The press conference with the Senator was broadcost on television.

參議員的記者會在電視上播放。

2. The reporters questioned the President about foreign affairs at the press conference.

記者招待會上，記者們向總統發問有關國際事物。

※30. pull one's leg

〔註〕：【非正式】用語。開玩笑；作弄；愚弄別人。

例1. Don't pulling my leg.

別開我玩笑。

2. For a moment,I actually believed that his wife had royal blood.Then I realized he was pulling my leg.

起先我還真相信他太太有皇族血統，後來我才知道他在作弄我。

※31. pull over

〔註〕：靠邊停車。電影片中常看到巡邏警車把超速或違規車輛攔截，命其停車。

例1. The police man told the speeder to pull over.

警察告訴超速者靠邊停車。

2. Everyone pulled over to let the ambulance pass.

每個人把車靠邊，讓救護車先過。

※32. pull off

〔註〕:【非正式】用語,指做成功,尤指被認為不可能的或困難的事。To succeed in something thought difficult or impossible。

例:Ben Hogan pulled off the impossible by winning three golf tournments in on. year.

Ben Hogan一年內贏得3次似乎不可能的高爾夫球賽。

※33. push-up

〔註〕:俯地挺身,鍛鍊手臂和肩膀的運動。

例:The football team does push-ups every day.

橄欖球隊員每天做俯地挺身的運動。

34. put down

〔註1〕:鎮壓,以武力制止。

例:In 24 hours the General had entirely put down the rebellion.

將軍在24小時內已完全地把判軍鎮壓。

〔註2〕:同write down,記錄下來。

例:He put down the story while it was fresh in his mind.

當還記憶猶新時,他把故事記下來。

※35. put off

〔註〕:延期;延遲,即postpone

例:We put off the picnic because of the rain.

因為下雨,我們把野餐延期。

※36. put on

〔註1〕:穿上衣服。

例：John took off his clothes and put on his pajama.
John脫下衣服，穿上睡衣。

※〔註2〕：開玩笑，取笑，為常用口語，必記。揶揄，嘲弄，Tease。

例：You put me on.
＝You're kidding me.
＝You are joking.
＝You're pulling my leg.
＝You pick on me.
你開我玩笑，取笑我。（拿我開心）

37. put one's foot in one's mouth

〔註〕：動詞片語。【非正式】用語。把腳塞到自己嘴巴，意指說話不經過大腦，即失言，失禮。所謂言之者無意，聽之者有意。

例：He put his foot in his mouth with his joke about the church,not knowing that one of the guests belonged to it.
他說的有關教會的笑話太失言了，因為他不知其中有客人屬於該教會。

38. put out

〔註〕：熄滅；撲滅。

例：The firemen put out the fire.
消防隊員把火熄滅了。

39. put out of the way

〔註〕：殺死，To kill。

例：When people spoke against the dictator, he

had them put out of the way.

當老百姓聲討獨裁者時，獨裁者把他們統統殺光。

※40. put up with

〔註〕：忍受；忍耐。

例：I can't put up with Bob's poor table manners.

我實在無法忍受Bob不雅的餐桌禮儀。

II. 常用短句，格言，句型練習

41. picture that!

明白了嗎！了解嗎！

〔註〕：picture當v.明白的描述。詢問別人對問題是否了解。

例：I've got the picture.

我明白了。

42. No one is perfect.

沒有人是十全十美的。

〔註〕：perfect是指美好的，棒極了。找男朋友或女朋友，只要品性良好，身家清白，肯上進就可以，不必一定要美麗，又有財富，學問又好，簡直是不可能，別傻了。

No one is perfect.

43. I promise

我答應

〔註〕：對別人所做的任何承諾。

※44. Don't play dumb with me

別跟我裝蒜。

〔註〕：別跟我裝傻。即Don't pretend you don't know what I'm talking about電視影集中cop質問嫌疑犯，其卻支吾其詞，左顧而言他。cop大怒，"Don't play dumb with me."少來，快從實招來，別跟我裝蒜，免受皮肉之苦。

※45. please say hello to your parents for me.

請代向令尊令堂問好。

〔註〕：常用客套問候語。Please say hello to＋someone（問候的人）。

46. We are pride of you

我們以你為榮。

〔註〕：因某人的傑出，而與有榮焉。

2-7 PART（Q）

Ⅰ. 常用口語

1. quick buck（或fast buck）

〔註〕：【俚語】。所謂的橫財，賺的又快又容易，不義之財。人無橫財不富，古今中外皆然，此乃人類貪婪的本性。君不信，大家樂，六合彩橫行，股票，房地產狂飆不正是最好的證明嗎？

2. I quit the job

我辭職不幹了。

〔註〕：quit為停止，中斷，停工。為常用口語動詞。I quit 我放棄，我不幹了。

PART（R）

Ⅰ．常用單字，俚語，俗語

※1. Really?

真的嗎?

〔註〕：表示驚訝，驚奇口語常用。

例：Q:We're going to Mexico this summer.

A:Oh,really?

問:今年夏天我們要到墨西哥去。

答:哦，真的嗎?

2. rear door

後門

〔註〕：如公共汽車的後門。rear mirrow車子後視鏡，rear end指車子的尾部。

例1. Open the rear door,please.

請把後門打開。

2. The rear end of my car was smashed.

我車子的尾部被撞了。

※3. rest room

洗手間，盥洗室

〔註〕：在美國洗手間，沒有用W.C.字眼，常用的有man room男廁，woman room女廁，或只寫man，woman而已。bath room指在家裡盥洗室，飛機上則用Lavatory，外出須特別注意，以免內急時找不到洗手間而受窘。

例：Excause me,where is the rest room.

對不起，請問盥洗室在那裡。

4. **Red tape**

打官腔，官僚作風

〔註〕：官僚作風，即Bureaucracy，公家機關的特色。

例：There is so much bureaucracy today.

今天有太多的官僚作風。

※5. **rush hour**

交通尖峰時間

〔註〕：特別是指上下班交通工具擁擠的時刻。traffic jam則是指交通阻塞，交通瓶頸。

例：Since it's the rush hour,Let's take the subway.

因是交通尖峰時間，我們搭地下鐵吧！

6. **room service**

客房服務

〔註〕：住旅館時的房間服務，包括像送早點，送換洗衣物等。

例：We called for room service when we wanted ice.

當我們需要冰塊時，我們就打電話叫客房服務。

※7. **rain check**

〔註1〕：【非正式】用語，常用口語。答應別人下次補請。

例1. I owed you rain check.

我下次再補請你。

2. It's too bad that you can't come to dinner this evening,I'll give you a rain check.
很遺憾今晚你不能來晚餐，我改天再補請你吧。

〔註2〕：因下雨而延期的比賽或表演留待日後再使用的免費入場券。

例：Manager told the crowd that they would be given rain checks for tomorrow's game.
經理告訴觀衆，他們可以得到明天比賽的免費入場券。

8. read one like a book

讀人如讀書

〔註〕：動詞片語，【非正式】用語。比喻知人之深，非常了解別人，所謂知己知彼，百戰百勝。

例：John's girl friend could read him like a book.
John的女朋友非常了解他。

9. regular guy（或regular fellow）

友善而隨和的人

〔註〕：【非正式】用語。指友善而容易相處的人。

例：You'll like Tom,He's a regular guy.
你會喜歡Tom的，他是個隨和的人。

※10. right away

立刻，即刻

〔註〕：副詞片語，Immediately。

例1. You have to do your homework right away.
你必須立刻做好你的家庭作業。

2. Bill knew the answer right away.

Bill很快就知道答案了

※11. right on

〔註〕：【俚語】，【俗語】。用以表示支持或讚成的呼叫附和，表示「同意」，「你說的對極了」，「完全正確」等。

例：Orator: And we shall see the pormised land!

Crowd: Right on!

演說者：我們將會看到希望的土地！

群衆：完全正確！（是的）

12. ring a bell

〔註〕：動詞片語。使你想起某事，似乎很熟悉。

例1. Q: Do you know Susan Flannigan?

A: That name ring a bell, but I'm not sure.

問：你認識Susan Flanningan嗎？

答：這名字很熟，但我不很確定。

※13. ring up

〔註1〕：超級市場結帳時，收銀機把總數加起來並記在收據上。

例：The supermarket cleark rang up Mrs. Smith's purchases and told her she owed $35.

超市職員把Smith太太購物總數加起來，告訴她一共三十五美元。

〔註2〕：【非正式】用語，指打電話。

例：Jenny rang up Sue and told her the news.

Jenny打電話給Sue，並告訴她這個消息。

14. road sign

〔註〕：路標，指示牌。高速公路上開車常看到的指

示牌，告訴駕駛人行車遵守的時速，方向等。

例1. The road sign said Boston was five miles away.
路標指示到波士頓有5哩路。

2. The road sign read,“55 MPH Limit” .
路標寫，“速度限制每小時55哩”。

15. road test

〔註〕：路考，測驗你是否能勝任開車。

例：Mary took the road test and got her driver's license last week.
上星期Mary考了路考，並取得駕照。

※16. rob the cradle

〔註〕：動詞片語，【非正式】用語。指老少配，與比自己年青很多的人約會或結婚。世風日下，男女平等，只要有錢有勢娶個年少美嬌娘不足為奇。開放的美國衆多半老徐娘嫁個年青小白臉更是蔚為風尚。老夫少妻，老妻少夫配。

例：When the old woman married a young man, everyone said she was robbing the cradle.
當半老徐娘婦人嫁給年青小伙子，大家都說她是老配少。

※17. rock'n'roll (rock and roll)

〔註〕：指搖滾樂，節奏輕快有力，又叫又吼的時下年青人最喜歡的玩意兒。

例：Rock'n'roll appeals mostly to young people.
搖滾樂吸引大部份的年青人。

18. rubber check

〔註〕：【非正式】用語，指支票跳票，支票不能兌現。

例1. The rubber check bounced.

支票拒絕往來（退票）

2. Bob got into trouble when he paid his bills with rubber checks.

Bob有麻煩了，當他付帳被退票時。

19. run away with

〔註〕：偷走，拿了就跑，steal

例：A theif ran away with Mary's necklace.

小偷偷走了Mary的項鍊。

20. run into

〔註1〕：偶然碰見。

例：I ran into Bob yesterday on Park street.

昨天在公園街我偶然遇見Bob。

〔註2〕：撞到，碰到。hit之意

例：Joe lost control of his bike and ran into a tree.

Joe的腳踏車失去控制而撞上了樹。

21. run short

〔註〕：動詞片語。短缺不足，用完了。

例1. We are running short of sugar.

我們沒有糖了。

2. We are out of potatoes and the flour is runing short.

我們馬鈴薯用完了，而麵粉也沒有了。

II. 常用短句，格言

22. Do you give refunds on empties?

空瓶子是否可退錢？

〔註〕：refunds是指退款。在美國有人是靠檢百事可樂或可口可樂鋁罐裝空瓶，或啤酒瓶鋁罐空瓶生活，一個大約可退5cent信不信由你，用後可不要隨便亂丟，有環保概念。目前國內也有推行，似乎效果不好。

※23. rolling stone gathers no moss

滾動的石頭不長苔

〔註〕：【格言】，比喻意志不堅定的人不會成功。

例：Bob was a rolling stone that gathered no moss. He worked in different jobs all over the country.

Bob是意志不堅定的人，他做過不同的工作幾乎遍佈全國。

PART（S）

Ⅰ．常用單字，俚語，俗語

※1. Sensational！

棒極了！

〔註〕：常用口語，sensational是激動感情的。看到女朋友打扮得花枝招展，趕快美言兩句。

例：You look sensational！

妳真漂亮極了！

※2. Shoot！（或speaking）

說吧！

〔註〕：常用於電話交談中，即有話快說吧！

※3. She

[ʃi]她（指女性第三人稱）

〔註〕：請特別注意發音。英語第三人稱男性he和女性的she，發音不同。雖然很簡單，但在實際會話時，中國學生時常弄混，故特別提出來提醒讀者。he[hi]，他。

例1. She is Mary.

她是Mary.（女性）

2. He is ready.

他準備好了。（男生）

4. sightseeing

觀光，遊覽

〔註〕：sightseeing tour觀光旅遊。sightseeing bus

觀光巴士。

例：Most of our time was spent in sightseeing.
我們大部份的時間花在觀光。

※5. soap opera

肥皂劇，電視連續劇

〔註〕：逐日連續播出的電視連續劇，大部份家庭主婦，一面工作，一面看soap opera。

6. Souvenirs

[ˌsuvəˈnɪr]

紀念品，紀念物

〔註〕：出國觀光或遊覽名勝最常購買的紀念物。

※7. sticker

粘貼標籤，粘貼紙

〔註〕：粘貼的標籤，如學生證後面所貼的小膠紙。

例：Place validation sticker on reverse side of photo ID card.
把有效的黏貼標籤貼在有照片身份證的背面。

8. shopping center

購物中心

〔註〕：美國大型購物中心都在郊區，附設有大的停車場而且各種貨品齊全，應有盡有。

例：All the stores in shopping center stay open until nine o'clock on Friday evenings.
所有商店的購物中心星期五晚上都營業到九點。

※9. So long

〔註〕：【俗語】，【非正式】，再見good-bye之意。常用於當與朋友分開道別時，互道再見。

其他類似常用的尚有，take care；see you ；take it easy。

例：So long,I'll be back tomorrow.

再見，我明天會再來。

※10. spoil ［spɔɪl］

〔註1〕：常用動詞，破壞；損害。

例：Jones joined the party and spoiled the pleasure of everyone by his impolite behavior.

Jones參加舞會，但他不禮貌的行為破壞了每個人的樂趣。

〔註2〕：寵壞；姑息。

例：They spoil their children.

他們寵壞了他們的小孩。

11. superbowl

超級盃美式足球大賽

〔 註 〕：全美國最熱門足球冠軍賽，該場比賽常吸引數萬觀眾觀賞。

※12. see

〔註1〕：v.t.看見，看到

例：Do you see that man？

你看見那個人嗎？

※〔註2〕：常用於口語，明白，瞭解，即I see之意，comprehend，明白，了解，知道。

例1. Q:How to open this beer can？

A:That's piece of cake,just pull the loop, see？

問：怎麼把這啤酒罐打開呢？

答：那太簡單了，只要拉開圈環，明白了嗎？

例2. I see your point.

我明白你的意思。

3. See what I mean?

明白我的意思嗎？

13. senior citizen

〔註〕：年齡超過65歲以上的老人或退休的人，美國政府都訂有各種優待，如乘車，飛機，各種福利優待等。

14. social security number

社會福利卡號碼

〔註〕：凡是美國公民，皆有此號碼，是工作，銀行開戶，或考駕照執照所必須的。留學生亦可申請，但上面加註不可工作的。

※15. so-so

馬馬虎虎

〔註〕：常用口語。馬馬虎虎，不好也不壞，普通。友人問你，近來股票大賺錢吧，可答之，so-so，有賠有賺，還過得去。

例Q:How is the test today?

A:So-so.

問：今天的考試如何？答：馬馬虎虎。

※16. sunny-side up

〔註〕：荷包蛋只煎熟一面，有如太陽一樣。如兩面都煎熟則是over easy。請務必記住。到餐廳用餐，尤其是早餐special，侍者會問，蛋要怎樣的吃法？

例1. Q:How do.you like your eggs?
A:Sunny-side up,please.(or over easy)
問:蛋要怎麼吃?
答:請煎一面吧。(兩面都煎)
2. Barbara likes her eggs sunny-side up.
Barbara喜歡她的蛋只煎一面的。

※17. Sure thing

當然的

〔註〕:【非正式】用語,即of course;certainly。當然的,毫無疑問的。

例:Sure thing.I'll be glad to do it for you.
當然,我很樂意為你效勞。

18. Sugar daddy

〔註〕:【俚語】,指凱子,有錢的老頭子。常給予年青的女孩子金錢或禮物以交換愛情。

例:Betty got a mink coat from.her sugar dady.
Betty從她老相好那裡得到貂皮大衣。

19. sales slip

銷售單據(售貨收據)

〔註〕:購物時,店員給你的小紙條,上面列有你購買的東西數量,金額名細等的銷售收據。

例:Mrs. Smith checked the sales slip with what she bought.
Smith太太核對購物收據。

20. save face

〔註〕:動詞片語,挽救聲譽,保留面子。死要面子不只是中國人的專利,中外皆然,可不必大

驚小怪。

例：The policeman was caught accepting a bribe; he tried to save face by claiming it was money owed to.him.

警察被捉到收受賄賂；但他宣稱是別人欠他的錢試圖保住聲譽。

※21. save one's breath

省省力氣，保持緘默

〔註〕：副詞片語。【非正式】用語。省省力氣，因多說也於事無補，說也沒有用。勸別人勿再白費力氣，以免徒勞無功。

例1. Save your breath;the boss.will never give you the day off.

省省力氣吧，老板不會給你休假的。

22. savings account

儲蓄存款帳戶

〔註〕：checkaccount，支票存款帳戶，可使用支票，還可辦提款卡。

※23. screw up

〔註〕：動詞片語。【俚語】，常用於口語。弄迷糊了，搞砸了。做錯使混亂或迷惑。

例1. Q:How about the test？

A:I screw up.

問：考得如何？

答：我搞砸了。

2. Her divorce screwed her up so badly that she had to go to psychiatrist.

離婚使她心情混亂，以致她必須去看精神科醫師。

3. It made me screw up.

它把我弄迷糊了。

※24. see someone off

〔註〕：送行；向某人道別。

例1. I'll see you off at the airport.

我到機場給你送行。

2. When Bob flew to New York,Mary saw him off at the airport.

當Bob飛到紐約時，Mary到機場給他送行。

25. sell out

銷售一空

〔註1〕：把存貨銷售一空。

例1. All sold out.

全部賣光。

2. In store's on sale the sheets and pillow cases were sold out in two days.

商店拍賣床單和枕頭罩兩天內銷售一空。

〔註2〕：清倉大拍賣，結束營業。

例：The local hard ware store sold out last month and was neplaced by a cafe.

本地五金店上月清倉大拍賣結束營業，由餐廳取代。

26. set out

〔註〕：旅行或航行出發。

例：The pilgrims set out for the New world.

清教徒啟航出發往新世界。

27. Set the world on fire.

做一番轟轟烈烈的事

〔註〕：動詞片語，【非正式】用語，把世界燃燒起來，比喻做一番大事業引人注目或使成名。

例1. Bob works hard,but he will never set the world on fire.

Bob很努力工作，但他並不很傑出。

2. Mary could set the world on fire with her piano playing.

Mary的鋼琴演奏，可能使她一舉成名。

※28. settle down

〔註〕：安頓下來；定居下來。

例1:John will settle down after he gets a job and get married.

John在找到一份工作和結婚以後將安頓下來。

※29. Set up

〔註1〕：建立；設立；establish。

例1. He has set up a new store recently.

他最近開設了一家新商店。

2. The government has set up many hospitals for veterans of the armed forces.

政府為陸軍退除役官兵設立了許多醫院。

※〔註2〕：作弄，整人，陷害某人。

例1. You set me up at the begining.

你一開始就陷害我。

2. He was set up.

他是被陷害的。

※30. short cut

〔註〕：1. 指捷徑。較近又便捷的路徑。

2. 做事的捷徑，攀龍附鳳是官場升遷的 short cut.

31. shake off

擺脫跟蹤

〔註〕：【非正式】用語。逃脫，擺脫別人跟蹤，摔掉。

例1. He shook off the stranger trying to follow him.

他擺脫想跟蹤他的陌生人。

2. She shake off a bad companion.

她擺脫了壞朋友。

32. show off

炫耀；展示。

〔註〕：炫耀，企圖引起注意。

例：John always show off his muscle when pretty girl move in next door.

當有漂亮的妞兒搬進隔壁，John常炫耀他的肌肉。

※33. show up

〔註〕：【非正式】常用口語，出現；出席。To come；appear。

例1. Only ten students showed up for class meeting.

只有十位學生出席會議。

2. We had agreed to meet at the Gym, but Bob didn't show up.

我們講好在體育館碰面，但Bob卻未出現。

※34. shut up

〔註〕：【非正式】用語。閉嘴，不要再講了，To stop talking。通常用於命令，語氣不太禮貌。

例1. Shut up and let Joe say something.
閉嘴，讓Joe說吧。

2. Oh,shut up ! I am tired of your talk.
哦，閉嘴，我受不了你嘮叨。

35. shut down

〔註〕：停止所有工作；完全停滯工作。

例：The company shut down the factory for Chrismas.聖誕節公司停止工廠的工作。

※36. sign in

〔註〕：簽到，簽名字在簽到簿上，表示出席。

例1. Every student must sign in when he comes back to the Dorm.
回到宿舍時，每位學生都必須簽到。

2. Teachers go to the office and sign in every morning.
老師每天到辦公室並簽到。

37. sign out

〔註〕：簽退，與sign in剛好相反。簽名字在簽名簿上表示離開。

例：Most of the students sign out on Friday.
大部份學生星期五簽退。

※38. sign up

〔註〕：註册；登記，即register常用於口語。學生

註册。

例1. Bob wants to sign up for the competition.
Bob要登記比賽。

2. We will not have the picnic unless more people sign up.
除非更多人報名，否則我們將不舉行野餐。

39. skid row

〔註〕：貧民窟，不要以為美國遍地黃金，紐約的貧民窟若非親眼目睹，真不敢相信。

例：The Bowery is New York City's skid row.
Bowery是紐約市的貧民區。

※40. slow down

〔註〕：把車子減速慢行。常見於大馬路上十字路口，寫著的斗大字。警告駕駛人減速慢行。

例1. Slow down, Smokey's ahead!
減速慢行，前面有警察巡邏車！
（Smokey是警察，警察巡邏車，為較新俚語）

2. The road is slippery, you'd better slow down.
路很滑，你最好減速慢行。

41. speed up

〔註〕：加足馬力，加速快行，與slow down正好相反。

例：The car speed up when it reach the country.
當快到鄉村時，車子加速快行。

※42. smell a rat

〔註〕：【非正式】，【俗語】，感到懷疑，覺得某

事不對勁。

例：Every time Tom visit me,one of my books disappears.I'm beginning to smell a rat.
每次Tom拜訪我時，我的書就有一本遺失，我開始有些懷疑他了。

※43. so-and-so

〔註1〕：指某某人，沒有特定的人名。【非正式】用語。

例：Don't tell me what so-and-so thinks. Tell me what you think.
別告訴我某某人的想法，只告訴我你的想法。

※44. so for,so good

〔註〕：【俗語】，【非正式】用語，指到目前為止事情進行還算順利。

例1. So far,so good;I hope we keep on doing well.
到目前還好，我希望我們繼續做好。

2. So far,so good;I hope we keep on with such good luck.
目前還好，我希望我們一直好運。

※45. son of a gun

〔註1〕：名詞片語。【俚語】，指壞人，壞傢伙。混蛋。

例：I don't like John;keep that son of a gun out of here.
我不喜歡John這混蛋把他趕走。

〔註2〕：常用於口語，口頭禪。開玩笑，但不一定是

惡意。

例：Hello Bob, you old son of a gun！

喂Bob，你這老傢伙。

〔註3〕：用於表示驚訝或失望。

例：Son of a gun！I lost my car keys.

糟了！我遺失了車子的鑰匙。

46. sooner or later

〔註〕：副詞片語，遲早總會發生的。

例：Study hard, or you'll repent it sooner or later.

努力用功，否則遲早你會後悔的。

※47. so what

〔註〕：【非正式】用語。是又怎麼樣，有什麼了不起，不屑一顧的樣子，為較不禮貌的回答。

例：Bob boasted that he was in the sixth grade, but John said,"So what？I'm in junior high."

Bob吹牛說他是六年級，但John說："是又怎麼樣，我是高年級。"

※48. speak up

〔註1〕：大聲說出或清楚說出。即speak out

例1. What's on your mind？Speak up！

你有什麼心事？說出來吧！

2. The teacher told the shy boy to speak up.

老師告訴害羞的男孩，大聲說出話來。

〔註2〕：聲言支持或反對某人或某事。

例1. Bob spoke up for John as student president.

Bob聲言支持John當學生會長。

※49. stand by

〔註1〕：候補；替補；當某人缺席時暫時替補。

例：Bob stood by with a fire extinguisher while the trash was burning.

當垃圾正燃燒時，Bob替補為消防隊員。

〔註2〕：支持，忠於，幫忙

例：Some people blamed Susan when she got in to trouble,but John stood by him.

當Susan有麻煩時，有些人責怪她，但John卻支持他。

50. stand for

〔註〕：代表…意義，想到。

例1. Our flag stands for our country.

我們的國旗代表國家。

2. The letter ″R.O.C″ stand for ″Republic of China.″

字母R.O.C.代表中華民國的意義。

51. stand out

〔註〕：顯得突出，鶴立雞群。比周圍環繞的人更高，更大或更好。

例：Jack was very tall and stood out in the crowd.

Jack很高在群衆中顯得突出。

52. stand up

〔註〕：起立。

例：Stand up,please.

請起立。

Sit down,please.（或Please be.seat;Take a seat）

請坐下。

※53. stay put

〔註〕：**【俗語】**，口語時常用，即stay where you are，不要離開；停在原地別走開；繼續逗留。

例1. Bob's father told him to stay put until he came back.

Bob的父親告訴Bob，在他回來前別走開。

例2. You stay put and don't make any noise.

你呆在這裡不要吵。

例3. This is I.C.R.T,we'll have a new song for you,stay put,Okay?

這是台北社區電台，我們將為你播出新歌，別走開好嗎？

54. step down

〔註1〕：下台，離開公職或某重要職位，辭職。例如菲律賓前獨裁總統馬可仕，終為人民所摒棄而下台。

例：When president Macos lost his election. he had to step down.

當馬可仕總統選舉失利，他必須下台。

〔註2〕：從高處走下

例：When the greyhound bus stopped, the conductor stepped down to help the passengers.

當灰狗巴士停車時，車掌下來幫忙旅客下車。

55. stick around

〔註〕：【非正式】，【俚語】。指逗留在附近或等待。

例：Father tell me to stick around and we will go swimming.

父親告訴我不要走開，我們要去游泳。

※56. sticky weather

〔註〕：指hot and high huminity，溫熱的天氣渾身上下黏濕濕的，很不舒服的，像台北七，八月的天氣。

※57. stick out

〔註〕：【非正式】用語，堅持到底，有始有終。不管事情多久多艱難，直到做成功為主。通常以stick it out片語使用。

例1. English is hard,but if you stick it out you will speak very well.

英文很難，如果你堅持努力你會說得很好的。

2. John doesn't have a chance of winning the marathon,but he will stick out the race even if he finishes last.

John沒有機會贏得馬拉松比賽，即使最後一名跑完全程，他還是堅持到底。

58. stick up

〔註〕：【非正式】用語，持槍搶劫，同Hold up，電視或電影片中常見歹徒持槍搶劫的用語。

例1. Don't move! This is a stick up!
別動，這是搶劫。
2. Mr. Smith was the victim of a stick-up last night.
Smith先生是昨晚搶劫的受害者。

※59. stop by（或Drop by）

〔註〕：順道拜訪，或短暫的拜訪。

例1. Don't forget to stop by at the gas station.
別忘了順道到加油站去。
2. Drop by any time you're in town.
到鎮上來時，隨時歡迎順道拜訪。

※60. stop over

指停留在某地過夜或旅行途中短暫停留

〔註〕與stop by略有不同。

例：When we came back from Boston, we stopped over one night at New York.
當我們從Boston回來時，我們在紐約停留一夜。

61. strike out

〔註1〕：常用於棒球比賽術語，三陣出局，即打擊手擊球三次沒有擊中被判出局，棒球迷不可不知。

例1. The pitcher struck out three men in the game.
比賽中投手把參人給三陣出局。
2. The batter struck out twice.
打擊手被兩次三陣出局。

〔註2〕：開始嘗試一種新的工作或經驗。

例：John quit his job and struck out on his own as a traveling salesman.

John辭掉他的工作，開使嘗試當旅行推銷員。

II. 常用短句，格言，句型練習

※62. Sorry to have bother you,I know you're busy.

很抱歉打擾你，我知道你很忙。

〔 註 〕：對於打擾別人感到不安的客套話。

※63. What is this stuff ?

這是什麼東西？

〔 註 〕：stuff這個字非常廣用，可指任何東西，像食品，書籍等。請務必記住。

※64. seeing is believing

〔 註 〕：百聞不如一見。行萬里路勝讀萬卷書。

65. Send him in

請他進來吧

〔 註 〕：秘書小姐告訴老板有人求見，老板回答Send him in。

66. We sing the same song

我們志同道合。

〔 註 〕：唱相同的歌，表示志同道合。

67. Excuse me,somebody sit here？（或May I take this seat？）

對不起，這位子有人坐嗎？

〔 註 〕：假如無人佔用可答go ahead，請便。

※68. So do I.

我也是；我也一樣。

〔註〕：對別人的提議或意見表示認同。

例Q:It's so hot today,I wish there were a fan in the library.

A:So do I,I'll fall asleep.

問:今天太熱了，真希望圖書館有一部電扇。

答:我也一樣想，我快睡著了。

69. Speak of the devil and he appears.

〔註〕：【格言】同中文「說曹操，曹操就到」。即當談到某人時，某人就出現。

例：We were just talking about Bill when he came in the door. Speak of the.devil and he appears.

當我們正談論Bill時，他就出現在門口，真是說曹操，曹操就到。

70. Can you sneak out for a couple hours for shopping?

你可以溜出來幾個鐘頭逛街嗎？

〔註〕：sneak是潛行之意，溜出來，溜班。

71. I can't stand it any more.

我再也無法忍受了。

〔註〕：stand當忍受。對別人的行為無法忍受。

72. See you around

〔註〕：再見，同See you later；So long。當與朋友分離時用語。

※73. I'm serious.

我是說正經的；我是說真的。

〔註〕：serious為常用字，指嚴肅的，正經的，真的。

PART（T）

Ⅰ·常用單字，俚語，俗語

1. T.V. talk-show

電視脫口秀。

〔註〕：電視主持人耍嘴皮說笑話，取悅觀衆，很受多數美國人歡迎。

2. Term paper

學期報告。

〔註〕：美國大學中，期中或期末短篇的學期報告。美式教育注重學生獨立思考，有時除了課堂上課題材的考試以外，講師（instructor）還會要求學生交Term paper研究報告。
Research paper研究報告。
Thesis碩士論文。
Dissertation博士論文。

※3. terricfic !

太棒了！太完美了！

〔註〕：【非正式】常用口語。即very good；excellent之意。

例1. It's terricfic.
太棒了。

2. a terricfic idea.
很好的主意。

※4. Token

〔註〕：銅幣。坐地下鐵，公共汽車常用的特製代用銅幣。

例：Tokens are use on the subway and can be bought at underground station.
代幣只用於坐地下鐵，可以在地下鐵車站買到。

5. Toll Fee

〔註〕：高速公路的過路費。

6. touch down

〔註1〕：美式足球比賽達陣得分。即持球者越過對方球門以球觸地得分。

〔註2〕：飛機，太空梭等著陸。

※7. touching

〔註〕：adj.感動人的，引人傷感的。

例：It's a very touching story.
這是非常動人的故事。

※8. tough

〔註〕：常用口語，指困難，強壯，了不起。

例1. It's a tough job.
這是件困難的工作。

2. He is tough.（He is good）
他很了不起。

※9. Top dog（同Top banana）

〔註〕：【俚語】，【俗語】。指任何事業或組織的龍頭，老大或最有影響力的人。

例：Who's the top dog（banana） in this outfit?
（＝Whe is the boss in the place.）
誰是這商業機構的負責人（老板）?

10. Too bad

〔註〕：太糟了，太可惜了。表示惋惜之意。

例：It's too bad that we missed the circus.

我們錯過了馬戲團的演出太可惜了。

11. though

〔註〕：放在句尾，表示輕微的否定，although。

例Q:Mary sounds very strick teacher.

A:She certainly was ! She was a great teacher,though.

問：Mary似乎是嚴格的老師。

答：她確實是，但她是一位很棒的老師。

12. trouble maker

〔註〕：指搗蛋鬼。製造麻煩的人。

例：He is a trouble maker.

他是位搗蛋鬼。

※13. Take a.chance

〔註〕：動詞片語。常用口語，指碰碰運氣，接受失敗的冒險，可能會失敗，但也要試一試，「愛拼才會贏」。

例：We will take a chance on the weather.and have the party outdoor.

在這種天氣舉行室外宴會，我們有點碰運氣。

14. Take a good look

〔註〕：好好看一眼，仔細瞧瞧。

例：Hey you gusy-take a good look at this.

喂，各位，請仔細瞧瞧這是什麼。

15. Take a shower

〔註〕：洗淋浴澡，美式浴室通常用蓮蓬頭沖浴，即方便又容易。

例：I want to take a shower.

我要去沖浴了。

※16. take advantage of

〔註1〕：片語，利用；利用機會。常用於口語。

例：Mary took advantage of the lunch hour to finish her homework.

Mary利用吃中飯時間，作完家庭作業。

〔註2〕：指佔別人便宜，欺騙；詐欺。

例：He took advantage of his friend's kindness.

他佔盡他朋友仁慈的便宜。

17. take after

〔註〕：相似；相像。指因親族關係而相像。

例：He takes after his father in mathematical ability.

他在數學方面的能力和他父親一樣。

18. take aim

〔註〕：瞄準目標。射擊時對準目標。

例1. Be ready to shoot when the captain orders "Take aim."

當隊長下令"瞄準"時，就準備射擊。

2. He took careful aim.

他小心瞄準目標。

19. take at one's word.

〔註〕：相信別人所說的話，聽信某人之言。

例：If you say you don't want this coat, I'll

take you at your word and throw it away.
如果你說你不要這件大衣，我會相信你而把它丟掉。

20. take back

〔註〕：改變或否定先前的諾言或主意，否認，取消，收回。

例：I take back my offer to buy the house now that I've had a good look at it.
仔細看過房子以後，我取消先前要買的主意。

※21. take care

〔註1〕：保重。常用口語，當與朋友分開道別時用語。

例：Take care, Bob.
Bob保重。

〔註2〕：小心，謹慎。

例：We must take care to let nobody hear about this.
我們必須小心不要讓任何人聽到。

22. take care of

〔註1〕：動詞片語。照顧。

例：Mary stayed home to take care of the baby.
瑪麗留在家裡照顧小嬰兒。

※〔註2〕：【非正式】用語，處理；對付。同To deal with

例：I will take care of that letter.
我會處理那封信。

23. take down

〔註〕：記錄下來，抄寫下來。

例：I'll tell you how to get to the station; you had better take it down.

我告訴你怎麼到車站；你最好記下來。

24. take effect

〔註〕：片語，開始作用，生效。

例：It was nearly an hour before the sleeping pill took effect.

將近1小時安眠藥丸才會開始作用。

※25. take for granted

〔註〕：認為理所當然，視為當然。

例1. Bob took for granted that the invitation included his wife.

Bob認為接受邀請包括他太太是理所當然的。

2. He spoke English so well that I took it for grauted that he was an American.

他英語說得很好，因此我認為他當然是美國人。

※26. take into account

〔註〕：考慮，包括，計算在內。

例Q:How much time will we need to get to the lake?

A:You have to take the bad road into account.

問:要多久時間我們才能抵達湖邊?

答:你必須把不好的路程也計算在內。

※27. take it easy

〔註1〕：【非正式】常用語；謹慎；小心。take things easy.

例1. Take it easy,the roads are icy.
小心，路面結冰很滑。

〔註2〕：放輕鬆，別太緊張。

例1. Take it easy,buddy！
老兄，放輕鬆吧！

2. Barbara likes to take it easy.
Barbara喜歡放輕鬆。

※28. take it or leave it

〔註〕：【非正式】用語，表示接受某事或拒絕，即 yes or no，通常用於命令。要不要，不要就拉倒吧！

例：Bob said the price of the house was $30,000,take it or leave it.
Bob說這房子售價3萬美元，要不要。

※29. take off

〔註1〕：指飛機起飛。

例：Three airplanes took off at the same time.
三架飛機同時起飛。

〔註2〕：脫去，除去外衣，褲子。

例：Take off your coat when you get into the room.
當進入室內時，把外衣脫掉。

〔註3〕：【非正式】用法，摹仿別人的習慣動作或講話。

例：He make a career of taking off famous people for night club audiences.
他在夜總會以摹仿名人動作為業，取悅觀衆。

※30. take one's time

〔註〕：不用急，慢慢來。

※例1. Take your time,I am not hurry.

別急，我不趕時間。

2. It's better to take your time at this job than to hurry and make mistakes.

做這工作最好慢慢來，總比快而錯誤百出好。

31. take over

〔註〕：接管，負責，take charge。

例1. He expects to take over the business when his father retires.

他父親退休後，他希望接管他父親的事業。

32. take part

〔註〕：動詞片語，參與；加入，分享。

例：The Swiss did not take part in the two World Wars.

瑞士沒有參加兩次的世界大戰。

※33. take place

〔註〕：動詞片語。發生某事或舉行。

例：The accident took place only a block from his home.

意外發生在離他家只有一條街的地方。

※34. take potluck

〔註〕：動詞片語。potluck是一種客人自己帶食物，然後與主人朋友一起分享的聚會。大部份老中剛抵美國總會有culture shock之感，以為主人太小氣了，其實只是文化差異之故。

take potluck是指便餐，沒有特別準備豐盛的菜餚。

例1. You are welcome to stay to dinner if you will take potluck.
如果你不介意便餐，歡迎留下來吃晚飯。

35. take sides

〔註〕：動詞片語。加入辯論或爭吵的一方。

例1. Switzerland refused to take sides in the two World Wars.
在兩次世界大戰瑞士都拒絕加入任何一方。

2. Tom wanted to go fishing.Dick wanted to take a hike.Bob took sides with Tom.
Tom要去釣魚，Dick要去遠足，Bob加入Tom的行列。

※36. take turns

〔註〕：動詞片語。輪流；交換。

例：Ted and Bob took turns at digging the hole.
Ted和Bob輪流挖洞。

37. talk back (answer back)

〔註〕：【非正式】用法，頂嘴；反唇相譏。

例：George talked back when his.mother told him to stop watching television;he said,"I don't have to if I don't want to."
George的母親告訴他不要看電視，George卻頂嘴說「我不要就不要。」

38. teach a lesson

〔註〕：教訓某人

例：When John pulled Sally's hair,she taught him a lesson by breaking his toy.
當John拉扯Sally的頭髮，Sally把他的玩具弄壞來教訓他。

※39. tell apart

〔註〕：動詞片語。區別；辨別。

例：The teacher could not tell the twins apart.
老師不能區別這對雙胞胎。

※40. tell off

〔註〕：【非正式】常用口語。責備；數落某人。

例1. Q:I really told him off.He knew I was right,too.
A:Who did you tell off？
Q:My boss.
問：我可真好好的數落了他一番。他也知道我是對的。
答：你數落了誰？
問：我的老板。

2. Mr. Black got angry and told off the boss.
Black先生生氣而數落了他老板一番。

※41. tell you what（即I'll tell you what）

〔註〕：常用口語，即Here is an idea.我有好主意；我有辦法。

例：The hamburger stand is closed.Tell you what,Let's go to my house and cook some hot dogs.
漢堡店關門了。我有個主意，到我家弄些熱狗吃吧。

※42. that is (that is to say)

〔註〕：即是，換句話說。與I mean同義。

例：John is.a New Yorker；that is,he lives in New York.

John是紐約人，換句話說，他住在紐約。

※43. The more…,the more.

〔註〕：常用口語，愈…則愈。

例1. The more you eat,the fatter you will get.
你愈吃你會愈胖。

2. Get your report in when you can;the sooner, the better.
儘早交出你的報告，愈快愈好。

44. the matter

〔註〕：用於疑問或否定

※例：Why don't you answer me？What's the matter with you？

為什麽不回答我？到底怎麽了？（那裡不對勁了）

※45. think over

〔註〕：慎重考慮，仔細考慮。

例1. We'll think over your proposal.
我們會慎重考慮你的建議書。

2. Bob:Mary,I love you,would you marry me?
Mary:I don't know.Give me more time to think it over.
Bob:Mary我愛妳，嫁給我吧！
Mary:我不知道，給我一些時間仔細考慮一下吧！

46. throw a party（Hold a party）

〔註〕：動詞片語。【非正式】用語，舉行舞會。一般在美國party並不是我們想像中只是跳舞，吃點心而已，通常正式的party還得正經八百的穿著西裝打領帶，享受美食，認識朋友，聊聊天的社交活動。

例：The seniors threw a masquerade party on Halloween.

高年級同學萬聖節辦了化裝舞會。

※47. throw away

〔註〕：丟開，把不必要的東西丟棄。

例1. I never save those coupons;I just throw them away.

我未曾收集留下優待券，我把它們全部丟掉。

2. She threw away a good chance for a better job.

她放棄一個好工作的機會。

※48. throw up

〔註〕：【非正式】常用口語，暈車，暈船或不舒服時嘔吐，作嘔。vomitting嘔吐，常用於醫學名詞。

例1. He throw up！

他嘔吐了。

2. He took the medicine but threw it up a minute later.

他服藥後不久就嘔吐出來了。

49. Time will tell

〔註〕：時間將會證明一切。善有善報，惡有惡報，不是不報，日子未到。

※50. time out

〔註〕：指比賽中暫停，如球類比賽時，教練大叫 Time out！暫停。

例：The player called time out so he could tie his shoe.

球員叫暫停，以便他綁鞋子。

51. to one's face

〔註〕：副詞片語，當著某人的面，當面。

例：I told him to his face that I didn't like the idea.

我當面告訴他，我不喜歡這主意。

52. trade in

〔註〕：交易，以部份物品當交易的部份付款。

例：The dealer took our old car as a trade in.

經銷商把我們的舊車當做交易付款的一部份。

※53. trial ballon

〔註〕：政治術語。試探氣球，指利用一個行動方針試探人們的反應。政治人物最喜歡玩的花樣。

例：John mentioned the class presidency to Bob as a trial balloon to see if Bob might be interested in running.

John向Bob提到學生會長的事當試探氣球，看Bob是否有興趣競選。

※54. try on

〔註〕：指試穿衣服，鞋子…等是否合適。逛百貨公司department store時常會用到。

Q:Excuse me,Can I try this coat on?

A:Sure,go ahead!

問：對不起，我可試穿這件大衣嗎？

答：當然可以，請便！

※56. tune in

〔註〕：轉台，即調整收音機（radio）或電視機（television）到某個電台。

例：Tom tuned in to channel 3 to hear news.

Tom把頻道調到第3台收聽新聞報導。

※56. tune up

〔註〕：汽車進保養場常用語。指汽車引擎各部的滑潤調整，保養等。

例1. He took his car to the garage to have the engine tuned up.

他把車開到修車廠保養。

2. Father says the car needs a tune-up before winter begins.

父親說冬天來臨前車子須要保養。

※57. turn down

〔註〕：拒絕接受；reject；refuse to accept

例1. He turned it down.

他拒絕了。

2. His request for a raise was turned down.

他要求加薪被拒絕了。

58. turn in

※〔註1〕：交出，繳交給某人；同hand in。

例：Professor want me to turn in a good term paper.

教授要我交一篇好的學期報告。

※〔註2〕：【非正式】用語，指上床睡覺；To go to bed.

例1. He gets up early,and turns in early.

他早睡早起。

2. We were tired,so we turned in about ten o'clock.

我們累了，所以十點就上床睡覺。

※59. turn on

〔註1〕：指打開電燈，電視等。turn off正相反，把電燈，電視等關閉。

例1. He turned on the light.

他把燈打開。

2. Jack turned on the water.

Jack打開水龍頭。

※〔註2〕：【俚語】，指有吸引力，對於任何理想，人物，事物有很大興趣。

例1. She turn me on.

她把我給迷住了。(She's attractive)

2. Mozart's music always turns me on.

莫扎特的音樂常吸引我。

60. turn turtle

〔註〕：turtle是烏龜。烏龜翻倒，即upside down，上下顛倒。

例：The car skidded on the ice and turned turtle.
車子在雪地上滑行而翻倒了。

II. 常用短句

61. Thank you for coming.
謝謝光臨
〔註〕：主人對來訪客人表示謝謝。

62. That's my pleasure.
那是我的榮幸
〔註〕：對別人感謝你的幫忙客套的回答。

63. There you go again.
〔註〕：意思是「你又來這一套」。
男朋友向女友說些肉麻的甜言蜜語，女友反感隨即說出，There you go again你又來了。

2-8　PART（U）

Ⅰ．常用單字，俚語，俗語

※1．Um-hum

〔註〕：【非正式】用語，常用於口語回答時，等於「yes」之意，是的。

例1．Q:Are you going to the movies？
A:Um-hum.
問：你正要去看電影嗎？
答：是的。

2．Q:You just moved in this apartment,right？
A:Um-hum.
問：你剛搬進這公寓，是嗎？
答：是的。

※2．Up-to-date

〔註〕：最新的，最近的。Most recent；current。

例：An up-to-date American slang.
最新的美國俚語。

3．Upside down

〔註〕：顚倒，弄翻了，弄反了。

4．U-turn

〔註〕：U字型迴轉道，sharp turn是急轉彎。

例：It's clean,you can U-turn.
沒有來車，你可以迴轉了。

※5．underwear

〔註〕：指棉質的內衣褲。underclothes。

※6. upset

〔註〕：厭惡，討厭，對某人反感。常用口語。

例：I really upset.

我真的很反感（生氣）。

7. under a cloud

〔註〕：形容詞片語，指有嫌疑的，不被信任的。

例：Mary has been under a cloud since her roommate's bracelet disappeared.

Mary涉有嫌疑，因為她的室友項鍊不見了。

8. under arrest

〔註〕：形容詞片語。被警察逮到補了。

例：The man believed to have robbed the bank was placed under arrest.

被認為搶銀行的人被逮補了。

9. under the circumstances

〔註〕：副詞片語。即既存的情況下。在目前情況下。

例：Under the circumstances, Father couldn't risk giving up his job.

在目前的情況下，父親不可能冒險放棄他的工作。

※10. under the table

〔註〕：暗中進行的交易，即秘密交易。外交家最善長技倆，過去如前美國務卿季辛吉與中共的秘密穿梭外交即是。

例：She gave money under the table to get the position.

她暗中出錢取得職位。

※11. up to

〔註1〕：由…決定或選擇，depending on。

※例1. It's up to you.

由你決定。

2. I don't care when you finish the homework. It's up to you.

我不在乎你什麼時候寫完家庭作業，由你自己決定。

〔註2〕：正在做某事；doing。朋友見面寒喧常用語。

※例1. What are you up to？

正在忙些什麼？（你在做什麼）

（What are you doing right now？）

2. What are you up to with the matches, John？

John，你拿火柴想作什麼？

〔註3〕：直到；until；till。

例1. Up to now I always thought John was honest.

直到現在，我還一直認為John是誠實的。

※12. used to

〔註1〕：常用片語，習慣於，熟悉於。be used to.

例1. People get used to smoking and it is hard for them to stop.

人們習慣抽煙，對他們來說戒掉很難。

2. Farmers are used to working outdoors in the winter.

農夫們習慣冬天在室外工作。

〔註2〕：過去如此，表示過去的習慣，過去經常如此。過去曾經。

例1. I used to go to the movies often.
我過去常去看電影。

2. We don't visit Helen as much as we used to.
我們不再像以往常去拜訪Helen。

※13. use up

〔註1〕：用盡了，用完了。

例1. Don't use up all the soap.
Leave me some to wash with.
不要把肥皂用完，留些給我洗。

2. Jack used up his last dollar to see the movies.
Jack用完他最後的錢去看電影。

〔註2〕：【非正式】用語，很疲倦，累極了。

例1. After swimming across the lake, Robert was used up.
游過湖以後，Robert累死了。

PART（V）

I．常用單字，俗語

1．Valentine day

〔註〕：情人節，2月14日在西方亦稱作聖華倫泰節，因為這個節日是為了紀念古羅馬天主教大主教聖華倫而設立的。西洋人歡度情人節的方式，以送卡片居多，送卡片的對象者不限於情侶，夫妻，尙包括父母，兄弟，姊妹及親友等。

2．variety show

〔註〕：即電視綜藝節目，包括有各種不同的節目如唱歌，跳舞，喜劇，短劇等的entertainment。

3．vote down

〔註〕：投票反對；投票否決。

例：Congrass voted the bill down.
國會投票反對法案的通過。

4．vehicle ［'vilkl］

〔註〕：車輛，交通工具。

PART（W）

Ⅰ．常用單字，俚語，俗語

※1．weird！

不可思議的；奇異的；怪異的。

〔註〕：指他人行為怪異，行動荒誕，真是不可思議。

例：She is weid.

她很古怪。

※2．Welcome

〔註1〕歡迎

例1．Welcom to Taiwan.

歡迎到台灣。

2．We received a warm welcome.

我們受到熱烈的歡迎。

〔註2〕：當片語使用時，you're welcome。為常用口語。即對別人感謝，表示不用客氣。

3．well

〔註1〕：很好；好

例：He speaks English very well.

他英語說得很好。

〔註2〕：嗯！或好罷！口語時當介系詞，表示驚愕，同意，期待，允諾等溫和的感歎詞。

例1．Well,it can't be helped.

好罷，這是沒有辦法的。

2. Well,here we are at last.
好了，我們終於到了。
3. Well,who would have thought it?
啊，誰會想得到?

〔註3〕：對別人發問的問題無法即時回答，利用Well，拉長時間來思考。

例：Well,Let me see.
讓我想一想。

※4. workshop

〔註〕：a.指一組的人定期集合在一起互相討論研究的會。
b.一小組人的短期教育program解決特別問題。

5. wheels

車輛

〔註〕：【俚語】wheel原是輪子之意，指車子，同Car，Automobile，Vehicle。
wheelchair輪椅(病人坐用的)

例：Do you have wheels?
你有車子嗎?(同Vehicles；Cars)

6. waiting list

〔註〕：候補名單

例1. The landlord said there were no vacant apartments available,but that he would put the Rogers' name on the waiging list.
房東說沒有空房間可出租，但他將把Roger的名字放在候補名單上。

2. The nursery school enrollment was complete, so the director put our child's name on th e waiting list.
護校招生額滿，所以教務主任把我們的小孩名字列入候補名單。

※7. walk out

〔註1〕：突然離開。

例：He didn't say he wasn't coming back; he just walk out.
他沒說他不回來；他只是突然離開。

〔註2〕：罷工

例：When the company would not give them higher pay, the workers walked out.
當公司不給他們高薪時，工人們就罷工。

※8. wake up

〔註〕：起床，早上醒來。

例1. I usually wake up at 7:30, but this morning I overslep.
我通常7點30分起床，但今早睡過頭了。

2. Please wake me up at six.
請六點鐘叫我起床。

※9. warm up

〔註1〕：指運動前的熱身運動，暖身運動，常用於口語。

例1. The dancers began to warm up fiften minutes before the performance.

2. The coach told us to warm up before entering the pool.
教練告訴我們進游泳池前先要做熱身運動。

〔註2〕：溫熱食物，把食物再熱一下。

例：Mr. Jones was so late that his dinner get cold;his wife had to warm it up.
John先生太晚回來以致晚飯都涼了，他太太必須去溫熱一下。

10. walk on air

〔註〕：【非正式】用語，好像走在大氣中輕飄飄的感覺，即快樂又興奮。

例：Sue has been walking on air since she won the prize.
Sue因為贏得獎品，既興奮又快樂。

※11. watch out（＝Look out）

〔註〕：用於命令或警告。提醒別人小心，注意，留意。

例："Watch out！" John called,as the car came toward me.
當車子向我駛來時，John大叫「小心！」

※12. Waste one's breath

〔註〕：動詞片語。浪費口舌，力氣，即對別人苦口婆心而不為所動。

例1. I know what I want.You're wasting your breath.
我知道我想要的，你別浪費唇舌，我不會改變主意。

2. The teacher saw that she was wasting her breath;the children refused to believe her.
老師發現她白費力氣，因為學生不相信她。

※13. watch it

〔註〕：【非正式】用語，常用於命令。提醒別人小心注意。

例1. Watch it.—the bottom stair is loose!
注意，底層樓梯鬆了！

2. You'd better watch it.If you get into trouble again,you'll be expelled.
你最好小心！如果你再惹麻煩，你會被開除。

14. wear out

〔註1〕：穿壞了，用壞了。

例1. The old clock finally wore out.
這個舊時鐘終於用壞了。

2. The stockings are so worn out that they can't be mended any more.
襪子穿破到不能再修補。

〔註2〕：和tire out同義，使疲倦，累。

例：Don't wear yourself out by playing too hard.
不要玩得過度累壞自己。

15. wear out one's welcome

〔註〕：【非正式】用語。經常拜訪親友或停留太久，而變得不再受歡迎。

例1. This hot weather has worn out its welcome with us.
我們漸對熱天氣不喜歡。

2. The Smith children have worn out their welcome at our house because they never want to go home.
Smith家小孩到我們家不再受歡迎，因他們常賴著不回家。

16. wear the pants

〔註〕：動詞片語。【非正式】用語。穿褲子的，男人也。男尊女卑的大男人主義，指當家的，一家之主。

例：Mrs. Wilson talks a lot but Mr. Wilson wears the pants in their house.
Wilson太太話說得多，但在家裡還是Wilson先生當家。

17. weight down

〔註〕：荷重物使之下降；或太繁複而變得沒趣。

例1. The evergreens are weighed down by the deep snow.
長青樹由於被積雪覆蓋而下垂。

2. The book is weighted down with footnotes.
這本書加註了太多註解。(以致不太容易閱讀)

3. The T.V. program is weighed down by commercials.
電視節目加了太多商業廣告。

※18. What for?

〔註〕：對別人的行為，言論或動作表示疑問，常用於口語。

例1. What are you rinning for?

你為什麼要競選？

2. Bill's mother told him to wear his hat.
"What for？" he asked.
Billy的母親告訴他要戴帽子，他卻說，"為什麼？"

※19. What about？

〔註〕：常用口語，常單獨使用於問句，即concerning what，關於什麼事，有關什麼事。

例Q:I want to talk to you.
A:What about？
問：我想跟你談談。
答：關於什麼事？

※20. Why not？

有什麼不可以？

〔註〕：別人都如此做，我有什麼不可以。

※21. Wet behind the ears

〔註〕：形容詞片語。【非正式】用語，指沒有經驗的人，或涉世未深的年青人。即生手，菜鳥也。

例：The new student is still wet behind the ears; he has not yet learned the tricks that the boys play on each other.
新來的同學還沒有經驗，不知道男同學玩的詭計。

※22. Whether…or

〔註〕：通常用於間接問句。是否如何。

例：You must decide whether you should go or stay.
你必須決定是否離開或留下。

23. whispering campaign

〔註〕：政客最常使用的政治手段，即耳語，散佈不實的謠言以中傷對手。

例 ：A bad man has started a whispering campaign against the mayor, saying that he isn't honest.

壞人開始散佈謠言打擊市長，說他是不誠實的人。

24. Who's who

〔註〕：【非正式】用語，指名人。

25. work into

〔註〕：用力慢慢擠入，塞進去。

例 ：John worked his foot into the boot by pushing and pulling.

John用力推和拉把腳慢慢塞進雪鞋裡。

（〔註〕：boot是一種長統鞋子，內襯有絨毛保暖，在下雪天穿以禦寒。）

26. work on

〔註〕：作用在，使影響。

例：Senator Brown worked on the other committee members to vote for the bill.

Brown參議員的影響作用使其他委員投票通過法案。

※27. work out

〔註1〕：常用口語，指做運動。

例1. Work out books.

運動書籍。

2. He works out in the gym two hours every

day.

他每天在體育館運動兩小時。

3. This afternoon we went to the gym for a work out, we lifted weights.

今天下午我們到體育館運動，練習舉重。

〔註2〕：發現答案，找出答案。

例：John worked out his math problems all by himself.

John自己解答所有數學習題。

※28. wrap up

〔註1〕：【非正式】常用語，指完成工作；To finish a job。

例1. Let's wrap up the job and go home.

讓我們把工作作完回家。

〔註2〕：穿上暖和的衣服，To put on warm cloth es。

例：Mother told Mary to wrap up before going out into the cold.

母親告訴Mary寒天外出前要穿暖和一點。

II. 常用短句，格言，句型練習

※29. What's the big idea?

〔註〕：【非正式】用語，是否有什麼目的；用意，即居心何在。通常用於詢問不受歡迎的人或事。

例1. The Bob family painted their house red, white, and blue. What's the big idea?

Bob家人把房子漆成紅色，白色和藍色，到底是什麼用意？

2. I heard you are spreading false rumors about me, what's the big idea？

我聽說你在散佈我的謠言，到底有什麼目的？

※30. What's your priority？

你的首要目標是什麼？

〔註〕：priority是指優先權，重要性的順序。

31. What's more.

〔註〕：除此之外，還有更…。further more, besides。

例：Bob is a nice guy, what's more, he knows how to manage his business.

Bob是個大好人，除此之外他知道如何經營事業。

※32. What's going on？

到底怎麼回事了？

〔註〕：看到路上一大堆人圍觀，好奇的詢問可以用之。

33. Where are we？

我們到什麼地方了？

〔註〕：如車子坐了好長一段路，不知身在何處，詢問友人。

※34. Who is it？（Who is there？）

誰呀？

〔註〕：當有人敲門時，最好別立刻開門，先問清楚是誰，以免遇到歹徒。可以回答It's me, Tony是我，湯尼。

※35. What's the matter with you, John? Do you have problems?

John，你到底怎麽回事了？有什麽困難嗎？

〔註〕：看到別人神色不對，平時嘻嘻哈哈的，今天突然默默不語準是六合彩槓龜，不然就是被女朋友給甩了。可用之詢問所以然。

※36. What do you call this in English?

這東西英文怎麽說？

〔註〕：如發現不懂的東西，請教別人時。

37. What do you have in mind?

你有什麽計劃嗎？

※38. What happened to you?

到底發生了什麽事？

〔註〕：平時都準時上班，今天卻遲到關心的詢問到底什麽事延誤了。

例Q:What happened to you? You are so late.

A:My car is flat tire, and I had to walk.

問：到底發生什麽事？你遲到太久了。

答：我車子爆胎了，我必須走路。

39. What are you doing here?

你在此幹啥？

〔註〕：質問別人鬼鬼祟祟的，不幹好事。

※40. I give you my word.

我向你保證。

〔註1〕：word指諾言，保證。用來加強對方的信心

，是每天必用語。

例：I'm a man of my word.

我是守信的人。

〔註2〕：word當談話，所說的話。

例：May I have a word with you？

我可以同你談談嗎？（同對方談話之前，先徵得同意。）

※41. What's the significaut？

最重要的是什麼？

〔 註 〕：significaut 是 指 重 要 的important ，consequence。

42. When will you finish your program？

你什麼時候完成學位。

可以回答

I can't wait.

我等不及了。

〔註〕：完成學位是每一位莘莘學子的心願。

43. Wolf in sheep's clothing

〔註〕：偽君子也。狼披羊皮指偽善者。

例：Mrs. Black trusted the lawyer until she realized that he was a wolf in sheep's clothing.

Black太太一直相信她的律師，直到她認清他偽善的真象。

※44. Would you please hold the door open for me？

請替我把門打開著好嗎？

〔註〕：常用口語句型，Would you pleas＋……請，表示客氣。

PART (X)

1. X-rated

〔註〕：【俚語】，【俗語】，X級的，即限制級，指凡有關電影，雜誌，或書上判定為有色情的文字或圖片，只限於成人觀賞的。

例：Tom celebrated his 21st birthday by going to an X-rated movies.

Tom跑去看X級的電影，來慶祝他21歲生日。

PART（Y）

Ⅰ．常用口語單字，俚語，俗語

※1. you know,…（you know something）

〔註〕：口頭語連接詞，會話中常聽到。在跟別人說話之前用之。

例1. You know something,I've always take up painting.

你知道嗎？我一直想學繪畫。

2. You know,she is fired.

你知道嗎，她被解僱了。

※2. yellow pages directory

〔註〕：電話黃皮簿。通常美國電話簿分white pages是列一般住戶電話號碼和yellow pages則是列有電話號碼及依服務性質分類的廣告商號住址。

例：A listing of airlines can be found in the yellow pages.

航空公司的名單，可在電話黃皮簿上找到。

3. yes-man

〔註〕：名詞，【非正式】用語，指沒有主張，唯唯諾諾的人。即所謂乖乖牌。

例：John tries to get ahead on his job by being a yes-man.

John為了工作進展，只好當個唯唯諾諾的人。

4. yoo-hoo

〔註〕：感嘆詞，【非正式】用語，大聲喊叫以引人注意。特別是年青學生常用。

例：Bob opened the door and called, "yoo-hoo, Mother-are you home?"

Bob開門並大叫，「Yoo-hoo，媽，你在家嗎？」

※5. you bet

〔註〕：【非正式】用語，為每日必用。表示肯定的，是的，毫無疑問的，強調事實就是如此。

例1. You bet I would.

我會的。

2. You bet I didn't.

我沒有。

3. You bet I will be at the party.

我一定去參加舞會。

※6. you don't say

〔註〕：為感歎詞，【非正式】用語，用於表示對別人的發言感到驚訝，即「你不是說真的吧？」，真有點不敢相信之意。

例1. You don't say,do you?

你不是說真的吧，是嗎？

2. Q:Bill and Jean are going to get married.

A:You don't say!

問:Bill和Jean快結婚了。

答:真的嗎，你不是開玩笑吧！（真有點不相信，前不久他倆才鬧彆扭。）

※7. you do?

〔註〕：是嗎，真的嗎？把音調提高，對別人所提問題稍有懷疑。

例Q:I think that idea is terrific.

A:You do?

問：我認為那觀點太棒了。

答：真的嗎？（你真的這麼認為嗎？）

8. you do a very good job.

你把事情處理得很好。

〔註〕：對別人工作表示讚賞。

9. you said it

〔註〕：感嘆詞，【俚語】，表示對別人所說的話，強烈同意，有同意的看法，正是如此。

例1. Q:That sure was a good show.

A:You said it.

問：那真是一場精采的表演。

答：你說的沒錯，正是如此。（我同意你的看法）

2. Q:It sure is hot.

A:You said it.

問：真熱呀。

答：你說的沒錯。

※10. you're telling me

〔註〕：感嘆詞，【非正式】用語，表示事實很明顯無須再說明。或表同意，即「那還用說」

例1. Q:You're late.

A:You're telling me!

問：你遲到了。

答：我知道。（你別雞婆）

※11. you too

你也一樣

〔註〕：常用口語，即彼此，彼此。同same to you 。me too我也一樣。

例：Q:Have a nice day！

A:You too.

問：你好！

答：彼此，彼此。

PART (Z)

1. Zero in on

〔註1〕：【俚語】，關心，注意。

例1. The Senate zeroed in on the Latin-American problems.

參議院特別關注拉丁美洲的問題。

〔註2〕：指槍的歸零或對準目標。

例：American missiles have been zeroed in on certain targets,to be fired if necessary.

美國的飛彈正對準某特定目標，一有必要即發射。

2. zone defense

〔註〕：區域防守。籃球或美式足球比賽時，每位隊員守住一個區域。防止對方得分。

例：The coach tought his team a zone defense because he thought his players weren't fast enough to defend against individual opponents.

教練告訴隊員採區域防守，因他認為球員個別防守速度不夠快。

第三篇
美語三字經
你不可不知的粗話罵人俚語

為了禮節，一般的書籍都不鼓勵說，寫或研究某些為多數人禁止使用的字，像是涉及有關性或身體功能的字，像Fuck you！操××（幹××）之類。為了這個原故，標準的字典或學校上課時都很小心的把它刪除掉。但是人非聖賢，古今中外皆然，為了更真實的反應實際生活上部份美國人所說的英語，著者特別收錄一些日常生活中可聽到的市井之徒常用俗語，口頭禪，使你更了解真實的語言與真實的社會。知道了這些字的意義後，並不一定要去用它，但它會幫助你當看電影，電視影集時不再會有語言「話溝」，反而會因了解意義而會心一笑。下面為常聽到的美語三字經。

※1. Bastard

王八蛋，混蛋。

〔註〕：指私生子，雜種。憤怒時粗魯咒罵語。

※2. Bull shit！

狗屁不通。

〔註〕：老美表示討厭或不耐煩時常用語。有時只說Oh, shit！指 nonsense，無理的。

3. Bummber

飯桶，懶惰蟲。

〔註〕：〔俚語〕，指懶惰無用，不受歡迎的人。

※4. chicken

膽小鬼

〔註〕：〔俗語〕懦夫。數落別人膽怯，做事沒魄力，遇事畏縮不前。chicken out退縮，害怕。不過要罵人chicken時，可要當心被挨打。

5. cock

陽具同dick，男性生殖器。

〔註〕：醫學上正式用字是penis陰莖。

6. creep

不受歡迎的人。

7. clod

老粗，傻瓜

※8. damn you!

他媽的，去你的。

〔註〕：討厭或不高興時罵人的粗話，電影或電視影集常可聽到。或只damn！他媽的。

9. Dumb

愚笨的，笨蛋

〔註〕：〔俗語〕愚笨的

10. Dummy

愚笨的人，笨蛋，蠢蛋。

〔註〕〔俗語〕

※11. Fuck you

操××，幹××

〔註〕：最惡劣的咒罵語。幹××，有時只講Fuck，但是最好不要用以免惹禍上身。有時在年青人使用並不一定是惡毒的咒罵語，而是一種口頭禪。

Oh,Gee,Fucking car！唉啊好爛的車！

※12. God damn

他媽的

〔註〕：老美生氣或不高興時粗魯的咒罵語。

※13. jerk

愚笨的人，未經世故的人

〔註〕:〔俗語〕指笨拙或惹人討厭的傢伙。

14. klutz

愚笨或差勁的傢伙。

15. pussy

女性生殖器

〔註〕1. 醫學上使用female genitals

2. 〔俚語〕原是指毛茸茸柔軟之物，如pussy cat

※16. Shut up !

閉嘴!

〔註〕:〔俗語〕咆哮，對別人嘮叨不耐煩或不滿，不客氣的命令句，閉嘴。

例:Oh,shut up ! I am tired of your talk.

閉嘴，我聽厭了你的話。

※17. Son of a bitch

臭婊子

〔註〕:同Bastard，指私生子，婊子，惡劣的咒罵語。警匪槍戰影集中常可聽到歹徒破口大罵。

例:I'll kill you ! Son of a bitch !

我宰了你，臭婊子!

※18. Son of a gun

豈有此理，混蛋

〔註〕1. 〔俚語〕指壞人，王八蛋，不受歡迎的人。

例:I don't like Charley;keep that son of a gun out of here.

我不喜歡Charley;把這混蛋傢伙趕走。

2. 用於表示失望或驚訝

例：Son of a gun！I lost my car key！

糟了，我遺失了車鑰匙！

19．Sucker

傻瓜，笨蛋

〔註〕：〔俚語〕笨蛋，易受騙之人。

20．stupid

愚蠢的，笨的

〔註〕笨蛋。a stupid person罵人愚蠢無知。

21．turkey

〔註〕an imcompentent。指好出風頭卻沒有能力的人。

第四篇
附錄

4 — 1 美國人常用的姓和名字

4 — 2 常用縮寫字

4 — 3 機關商店名稱及相關用語

4—1 美國人常用的姓和名字

熟記別人的名字可以增加彼此間的距離。但是美國人的名字是把名字（The First name 或 give name）放在前面，姓（The Last name, surname或Family name）放在後面，卻好與中文相反。剛到美國往往為了填寫表格，弄得很迷糊，老美也搞不懂你的名字讀法，你也弄混了The last name（姓），The first name（名字）。下面提供一些美國人常用的姓和名字供參考。

【姓氏】

1. Smith
2. Gohnson
3. Brown
4. Williams
5. Millers
6. Jones
7. Davis
8. Anderson
9. Wilson
10. Taylor
11. Thomas
12. Moore
13. White
14. Martin
15. Thompson

【常用的名字】

Male男性

1. John
2. Willian
3. James
4. Robert
5. Charles
6. George
7. Willie

Female女性

1. Mary
2. Borothy
3. Helen
4. Margaret
5. Ruth
6. Betty
7. Elizabeth

8. Joseph	8. Anna
9. Frank	9. Mildred
10. Richard	10. Frances

4—2 常用縮寫字

1. Ad 廣告

〔註〕：Advertisment之縮寫，指報紙廣告或書面廣告。T.V.commercial指電視上的商業廣告。

2. AIDS 愛滋病

〔註〕：即Acquired Immune Deficience Syndrome又稱「後天免疫缺乏症候群」，是由愛滋病毒所引發的疾病。這種疾病會破壞人體的免疫系統，使人體失去抵抗疾病的能力，最後終於喪失寶貴的生命。一般是由同性戀者所引起。

3. A.B.C 華裔美國人

〔註〕：即American Born Chinese，指第二代在美出生的華裔美國人。俗稱Banana外表是東方黃臉孔，可是內在卻是白人思想。

4. B.Y.O 自備東西 〔註〕：Bring your own

5. C.I.A 美國中央情報局

※6. Dom 學生宿舍，Dormitory的簡稱。

7. D.J. 電台廣播員，Disc jockey

8. F.B.I 美國聯邦調查局 〔註〕Federal Bureau of Investigation

9. Gym 體育館 〔註〕：Gymnasium的簡稱。

10. High Tech 高科技（技術或產品）

11. I.D 身份證

〔註〕：Identification Card

12. I.O.U〔註〕：I owe you我欠你的。

13. K.G.B. 蘇俄公安部，是蘇聯的情報機構，冷戰時期常與美國情報局C.I.A.打對台。

14. Lab 實驗室。Language Lab則指語言視聽中心

15. M.A. Master of Art 文學碩士

16. M.S. Master of Science 理學碩士

17. MBA Master of Business Administration 企管碩士

18. NASA〔註〕：美國國家太空總署

National Aeronautics and Space Administration.

19. NATO〔註〕即北大西洋公約組織

North Atlantic Treaty Organization

20. OPEC〔註〕石油輸出國組織

Organization of Petroleum Exporting countries

21. GATT 關稅暨貿易總協定

General Agreement on Tariffs and Trade

〔註〕：GATT近來成為大家矚目的焦點，它的基本精神在於使GATT各會員國經由互惠互利的協商，削減關稅及其他貿易障礙，以期達到國際間，自由，公平的貿易往來，其組織勢力龐大，係為一個國際性的經貿組織。

22. U.F.O 幽靈飛碟

23. Pentago〔註〕：五角大厦，即美國國防部

24. Ph.D. 博士，即Doctor of philosophy

25. V.D.〔註〕：Venereal Disease性病

※26. T.G.I.F

〔註〕：Thanks god it's friday。美國一週上班五

天，星期五算週末，一到星期五特別高興。

4—3 機關，商店名稱及相關用語

1. Airport 飛機場

〔註〕常用相關用語

bridge空橋

baggages行李

control tower塔台

departure bilding航站登機處

terminal building機場大厦

passenger旅客

2. Aquarium水族館

3. Altalantic Casino大西洋賭城

〔註〕：美國的賭城是有名的觀光據點，像拉斯維加斯，除了可碰碰運氣賭一下，還有秀可看。賭城為招覽客人，不但坐車免費，還送現金。

slot machine 自動賭博機，即吃角子老虎

bank 莊家

player 賭客

roulette table 輪盤賭檯

4. Amtrak station 火車站

〔註〕one-way ticket 單程車票

Round-trip ticket來 回車票

timetable 時間表

Entrance 入口

date stamp 日期戳

baggage checking bureau 行李寄存處

5. Bank 銀行

〔註〕相關用語

savings account 儲蓄存款帳戶

Checking account 支票存款帳戶

wighdraw 提款

deposit 存款

interest 利息

pass book 存款簿

bank teller 銀行出納員

6. Book store 書店

7. Bakery 麵包店

〔註〕相關用語

popcorn 爆米花

cake 蛋糕

pie 餡餅，如 Apple pie 蘋果派

doughnut 甜甜圈

cookie 餅乾

8. Consulates 領事館

9. Department store 百貨公司

〔註〕：相關用語

cashier 出納員

escalator 電動扶梯

shopping cart 購物手推車

wrapping paper 包裝紙

※receipt 收據

10. Fastfood store 速食店

〔註〕：像麥當勞，漢堡王，肯德基炸雞店等。

11. garage修車廠

〔註〕相關用語

spare tire 備胎
jack 起重機，千斤頂
wiper 雨刷
front window 前窗
rear window 後窗
bumper 保險桿
carbureter 汽化器
battery 蓄電池
radiator 散熱器

12. gas station 加油站

〔註〕汽油分四種

regular 普通汽油
high test 高級汽油
unleaded 無鉛汽油
super unleaded 高級無鉛汽油
Fill it up,please 請加滿汽油

13. Galleries 美術陳列館，畫廊

14.Greyhund bus station 灰狗巴士車站

〔註〕Bus terminal 汽車總站

15. Hotel旅館，飯店

〔註〕相關用語

Front clerk 櫃檯服務員
lobby 候客大廳
register 登記簿。住旅館check in時要先登記
room key 房間鑰匙

single room 單人房
double room 雙人房
president suite 總統套房
check in 登記住進旅館
check out 結帳退房
reservation 預定

16. Hospital 醫院

〔註〕相關用語
Doc. 醫師 Doctor 負責疾病診斷
pharmacist 藥師，負責藥品調劑
Nurse 護士
patient 病人
clinical thermometer 體溫計
dentist 牙醫師
X-ray film X光底片
prescription 處方箋
wheel chair 輪椅

17. Hardware store 五金行，除了販賣五金以外，還兼賣雜貨

18. Liquor store 販賣酒的商店

19. pub 小酒館

〔註〕counter 櫃檯
cocktail 雞尾酒
waitress 女服務員
draught beer 生啤酒
cap opener 開瓶器

20. parliament 國會，議會

〔註〕speaker 議長
deputy speaker 副議長
auditor 旁聽人
congressman 國會議員
party in opposition 在野黨
party in power 執政黨
roll-call vote 點名投票
secretary秘書

21. pleasure ground 遊樂場

〔註〕遊樂場是小孩最喜歡的地方，像迪斯奈樂園則是老少皆宜的最佳去處。
merry-go-round 旋轉木馬
coffee-cup 旋轉咖啡杯
jet coaster 摩天輪
lift 吊纜車
money-exchange 兌錢處

22. post office 郵局

〔註〕相關用語
aerograms 郵筒
Registered Mail 掛號
Regular Mail 普通郵件
Certified Mail 雙掛號
special delivery 快遞
Zip code 郵遞區號
post card 明信片
air mail 航空郵件

23. pharmacy 藥局

〔註〕美式藥局一般規模很大。接受醫師處方調劑藥品外，兼賣雜貨等，如CVS，Sears 有很多連鎖店。也有兼沖洗照片收件服務。

develop 照片沖洗，使顯影

reprint 加洗照片

negative 底片

enlargement 照片放大

patient：May I have this prescription filled here?

I have a terrible headache.

pharmacist：yes. but you'll have a 10 minute wait.

病患：我可以在這裡調劑處方嗎？我頭痛得很厲害。

藥師：是的可以，但要請稍候10分鐘。

24. Restaruant大餐廳，大飯店

〔註〕相關用語

waiter侍者

menu 菜單

napkin 餐巾

beef-steak 牛排

salad 沙拉

spaghetti 通心粉

dessert 甜點

25. Symphany hall 交響樂音樂廳

26. Subway station 地下鐵車站

27. suppermarket 超級市場

28. campus 校園

〔註〕Instructor 導師
bulletin board 公佈欄
dormitory 學生宿舍
gymnasium 體育館
swimming pool 游泳池
professor 教授
locker 橱櫃
dining hall 餐廳

29. Gymnasium 體育館
相關用字basketball 籃球
volleyball 排球
server 發球者
Baseball 棒球
pitcher 投手
batter 打擊手
catcher 補手
inning棒球比賽，一局。
tennis court 網球場
soccer 足球
football 美式橄欖球

30. zoo 動物園
lion 雄獅
tiger 老虎
African elephant 非洲象
kangaroo 袋鼠
giraff 長頸鹿
puma 美洲豹

Zebra 斑馬
rhinoceros 犀牛
Ostrich 鴕鳥

大展出版社有限公司	圖書目錄

地址：台北市北投區11204
致遠一路二段12巷1號
郵撥： 0166955～1
電話：(02)8236031
8236033
傳眞：(02)8272069

・法律專欄連載・電腦編號 58

台大法學院 法律學系／策劃
法律服務社／編著

①別讓您的權利睡著了[1]		200元
②別讓您的權利睡著了[2]		200元

・秘傳占卜系列・電腦編號 14

①手相術	淺野八郎著	150元
②人相術	淺野八郎著	150元
③西洋占星術	淺野八郎著	150元
④中國神奇占卜	淺野八郎著	150元
⑤夢判斷	淺野八郎著	150元
⑥前世、來世占卜	淺野八郎著	150元
⑦法國式血型學	淺野八郎著	150元
⑧靈感、符咒學	淺野八郎著	150元
⑨紙牌占卜學	淺野八郎著	150元
⑩ＥＳＰ超能力占卜	淺野八郎著	150元
⑪猶太數的秘術	淺野八郎著	150元
⑫新心理測驗	淺野八郎著	160元

・趣味心理講座・電腦編號 15

①性格測驗１　探索男與女	淺野八郎著	140元
②性格測驗２　透視人心奧秘	淺野八郎著	140元
③性格測驗３　發現陌生的自己	淺野八郎著	140元
④性格測驗４　發現你的真面目	淺野八郎著	140元
⑤性格測驗５　讓你們吃驚	淺野八郎著	140元
⑥性格測驗６　洞穿心理盲點	淺野八郎著	140元
⑦性格測驗７　探索對方心理	淺野八郎著	140元
⑧性格測驗８　由吃認識自己	淺野八郎著	140元
⑨性格測驗９　戀愛知多少	淺野八郎著	140元

⑩性格測驗10	由裝扮瞭解人心	淺野八郎著	140元
⑪性格測驗11	敲開內心玄機	淺野八郎著	140元
⑫性格測驗12	透視你的未來	淺野八郎著	140元
⑬血型與你的一生		淺野八郎著	140元
⑭趣味推理遊戲		淺野八郎著	160元
⑮行爲語言解析		淺野八郎著	160元

・婦 幼 天 地・電腦編號 16

①八萬人減肥成果	黃靜香譯	180元
②三分鐘減肥體操	楊鴻儒譯	150元
③窈窕淑女美髮秘訣	柯素娥譯	130元
④使妳更迷人	成　玉譯	130元
⑤女性的更年期	官舒妍編譯	160元
⑥胎內育兒法	李玉瓊編譯	150元
⑦早產兒袋鼠式護理	唐岱蘭譯	200元
⑧初次懷孕與生產	婦幼天地編譯組	180元
⑨初次育兒12個月	婦幼天地編譯組	180元
⑩斷乳食與幼兒食	婦幼天地編譯組	180元
⑪培養幼兒能力與性向	婦幼天地編譯組	180元
⑫培養幼兒創造力的玩具與遊戲	婦幼天地編譯組	180元
⑬幼兒的症狀與疾病	婦幼天地編譯組	180元
⑭腿部苗條健美法	婦幼天地編譯組	150元
⑮女性腰痛別忽視	婦幼天地編譯組	150元
⑯舒展身心體操術	李玉瓊編譯	130元
⑰三分鐘臉部體操	趙薇妮著	160元
⑱生動的笑容表情術	趙薇妮著	160元
⑲心曠神怡減肥法	川津祐介著	130元
⑳內衣使妳更美麗	陳玄茹譯	130元
㉑瑜伽美姿美容	黃靜香編著	150元
㉒高雅女性裝扮學	陳珮玲譯	180元
㉓蠶糞肌膚美顏法	坂梨秀子著	160元
㉔認識妳的身體	李玉瓊譯	160元
㉕產後恢復苗條體態	居理安・芙萊喬著	200元
㉖正確護髮美容法	山崎伊久江著	180元
㉗安琪拉美姿養生學	安琪拉蘭斯博瑞著	180元
㉘女體性醫學剖析	增田豐著	220元
㉙懷孕與生產剖析	岡部綾子著	180元
㉚斷奶後的健康育兒	東城百合子著	220元

•青 春 天 地• 電腦編號 17

①A血型與星座	柯素娥編譯	120元
②B血型與星座	柯素娥編譯	120元
③O血型與星座	柯素娥編譯	120元
④AB血型與星座	柯素娥編譯	120元
⑤青春期性教室	呂貴嵐編譯	130元
⑥事半功倍讀書法	王毅希編譯	150元
⑦難解數學破題	宋釗宜編譯	130元
⑧速算解題技巧	宋釗宜編譯	130元
⑨小論文寫作秘訣	林顯茂編譯	120元
⑪中學生野外遊戲	熊谷康編著	120元
⑫恐怖極短篇	柯素娥編譯	130元
⑬恐怖夜話	小毛驢編譯	130元
⑭恐怖幽默短篇	小毛驢編譯	120元
⑮黑色幽默短篇	小毛驢編譯	120元
⑯靈異怪談	小毛驢編譯	130元
⑰錯覺遊戲	小毛驢編譯	130元
⑱整人遊戲	小毛驢編著	150元
⑲有趣的超常識	柯素娥編譯	130元
⑳哦！原來如此	林慶旺編譯	130元
㉑趣味競賽100種	劉名揚編譯	120元
㉒數學謎題入門	宋釗宜編譯	150元
㉓數學謎題解析	宋釗宜編譯	150元
㉔透視男女心理	林慶旺編譯	120元
㉕少女情懷的自白	李桂蘭編譯	120元
㉖由兄弟姊妹看命運	李玉瓊編譯	130元
㉗趣味的科學魔術	林慶旺編譯	150元
㉘趣味的心理實驗室	李燕玲編譯	150元
㉙愛與性心理測驗	小毛驢編譯	130元
㉚刑案推理解謎	小毛驢編譯	130元
㉛偵探常識推理	小毛驢編譯	130元
㉜偵探常識解謎	小毛驢編譯	130元
㉝偵探推理遊戲	小毛驢編譯	130元
㉞趣味的超魔術	廖玉山編著	150元
㉟趣味的珍奇發明	柯素娥編著	150元
㊱登山用具與技巧	陳瑞菊編著	150元

•健 康 天 地• 電腦編號 18

①壓力的預防與治療	柯素娥編譯	130元
②超科學氣的魔力	柯素娥編譯	130元
③尿療法治病的神奇	中尾良一著	130元
④鐵證如山的尿療法奇蹟	廖玉山譯	120元
⑤一日斷食健康法	葉慈容編譯	120元
⑥胃部強健法	陳炳崑譯	120元
⑦癌症早期檢查法	廖松濤譯	160元
⑧老人痴呆症防止法	柯素娥編譯	130元
⑨松葉汁健康飲料	陳麗芬編譯	130元
⑩揉肚臍健康法	永井秋夫著	150元
⑪過勞死、猝死的預防	卓秀貞編譯	130元
⑫高血壓治療與飲食	藤山順豐著	150元
⑬老人看護指南	柯素娥編譯	150元
⑭美容外科淺談	楊啟宏著	150元
⑮美容外科新境界	楊啟宏著	150元
⑯鹽是天然的醫生	西英司郎著	140元
⑰年輕十歲不是夢	梁瑞麟譯	200元
⑱茶料理治百病	桑野和民著	180元
⑲綠茶治病寶典	桑野和民著	150元
⑳杜仲茶養顏減肥法	西田博著	150元
㉑蜂膠驚人療效	瀨長良三郎著	150元
㉒蜂膠治百病	瀨長良三郎著	180元
㉓醫藥與生活	鄭炳全著	180元
㉔鈣長生寶典	落合敏著	180元
㉕大蒜長生寶典	木下繁太郎著	160元
㉖居家自我健康檢查	石川恭三著	160元
㉗永恒的健康人生	李秀鈴譯	200元
㉘大豆卵磷脂長生寶典	劉雪卿譯	150元
㉙芳香療法	梁艾琳譯	160元
㉚醋長生寶典	柯素娥譯	180元
㉛從星座透視健康	席拉・吉蒂斯著	180元
㉜愉悅自在保健學	野本二士夫著	160元
㉝裸睡健康法	丸山淳士等著	160元
㉞糖尿病預防與治療	藤田順豐著	180元
㉟維他命長生寶典	菅原明子著	180元
㊱維他命C新效果	鐘文訓編	150元
㊲手、腳病理按摩	堤芳郎著	160元
㊳AIDS瞭解與預防	彼得塔歇爾著	180元
㊴甲殼質殼聚糖健康法	沈永嘉譯	160元
㊵神經痛預防與治療	木下眞男著	160元
㊶室內身體鍛鍊法	陳炳崑編著	160元

㊷吃出健康藥膳	劉大器編著	180元
㊸自我指壓術	蘇燕謀編著	160元
㊹紅蘿蔔汁斷食療法	李玉瓊編著	150元
㊺洗心術健康秘法	竺翠萍編譯	170元
㊻枇杷葉健康療法	柯素娥編譯	180元
㊼抗衰血癒	楊啟宏著	180元

•實用女性學講座•電腦編號 19

①解讀女性內心世界	島田一男著	150元
②塑造成熟的女性	島田一男著	150元
③女性整體裝扮學	黃靜香編著	180元
④女性應對禮儀	黃靜香編著	180元

•校 園 系 列•電腦編號 20

①讀書集中術	多湖輝著	150元
②應考的訣竅	多湖輝著	150元
③輕鬆讀書贏得聯考	多湖輝著	150元
④讀書記憶秘訣	多湖輝著	150元
⑤視力恢復！超速讀術	江錦雲譯	180元

•實用心理學講座•電腦編號 21

①拆穿欺騙伎倆	多湖輝著	140元
②創造好構想	多湖輝著	140元
③面對面心理術	多湖輝著	160元
④偽裝心理術	多湖輝著	140元
⑤透視人性弱點	多湖輝著	140元
⑥自我表現術	多湖輝著	150元
⑦不可思議的人性心理	多湖輝著	150元
⑧催眠術入門	多湖輝著	150元
⑨責罵部屬的藝術	多湖輝著	150元
⑩精神力	多湖輝著	150元
⑪厚黑說服術	多湖輝著	150元
⑫集中力	多湖輝著	150元
⑬構想力	多湖輝著	150元
⑭深層心理術	多湖輝著	160元
⑮深層語言術	多湖輝著	160元
⑯深層說服術	多湖輝著	180元
⑰掌握潛在心理	多湖輝著	160元

國家圖書館出版品預行編目資料

學會美式俚語會話／王嘉明著，
—初版—臺北市，大展，民85
面；　公分—（語文特輯：20）
ISBN957-557-601-2（平裝）

1.英國語言—會話
2.英國語言—俗語、俚語

805.188　　　85004447

學會美式俚語會話

ISBN 957-557-601-2

著　者／王　嘉　明
發行人／蔡　森　明
出版者／大展出版社有限公司
社　址／台北市北投區（石牌）
致遠一路二段12巷1號
電　話／(02) 8236031・8236033
傳　眞／(02) 8272069
郵政劃撥／0166955－1
登記證／局版臺業字第2171號

承印者／國順圖書印刷公司
裝　訂／嶸興裝訂有限公司
排版者／千賓電腦打字有限公司
電　話／（02）8836052
初　版／1996年（民85年）6月

定　價／220元

大展好書 好書大展